The Devil You Know

James Schroeder

Published by James Schroeder, 2022.

This is a work of fiction. Similarities to real people, places, or events are entirely coincidental.

THE DEVIL YOU KNOW

First edition. July 5, 2022.

Copyright © 2022 James Schroeder.

ISBN: 979-8218040598

Written by James Schroeder.

This book is dedicated to my Grandpa,

(who unfortunately passed before its completion)

ACKNOWLEDGMENTS

I want to thank:

God. My Family (far too many to list at once). Hallie.

Those who helped look over the book: Marlene, Adam, Julie, Mary, Allen, Jake, Samir.

All the teachers who encouraged my writing over the years.

Draft 2 Digital,

and lastly, you, the reader.

Chapter 1

In the Gutter

Filth. It litters the streets of my city. Under every bench, in every alleyway, on every street corner, a new piece of trash somehow finds its way back onto the once-clean pavement. The more you try to clean one mess, another just takes its place. Before you know it, your hands are filthy. The dirtier they get, the more you want all the grime off of them, until you finally try to wash your hands of it. It's only then that you realize that while attempting to get rid of your mess, you need to dirty up something else, and the cycle continues again and again.

I've walked these polluted streets a thousand times. Every night, some new piece of trash turns up like a bad penny. I'm sure you know all too well that things seldom land softly when they've been tossed to the gutter. I've been kicked out of enough places where I can tell you from experience that the hard kiss of the pavement is far less pleasant than one from a dame; though, there are exceptions.

Too often or not, a man with a steady job and a positive outlook on life can find himself out on the curb among the rest of the trash. His good intentions and moral nature get flipped on his head until he's up to his neck in corruption. That kind of filth doesn't wash away with the rest of your dirty laundry. Soon, you're so far down the rabbit hole that you're stuck in the gutter.

All it takes is one bad day and the right devil to push you from the righteous path; one who'll keep his claws in you until he's tired of playing with you. And believe me, this city has plenty of devils to choose from—plenty more if you know where to look.

I walked down the drenched sidewalk in the pouring rain. I don't mind the rain. It's cool and washes the blood on my hands away; at least, on the surface. My trench coat was soaked and a steady stream of water flowed from the brim of my equally-soaked fedora to the city street below. I was so wet that I looked like I'd taken a dip in Lake Michigan. Even the dying embers of the cigarette pressed between my lips barely managed to stay lit in the downpour.

I was in no particular hurry and walked at a slow steady pace. The few souls who encountered me on the street kept a safe distance, some even ducked into shops and alleyways to avoid me altogether as I passed. I paid them no mind and continued on my way with the usual destination in mind; the bar.

I traveled down a long dark alley and continued down a narrow hallway until I reached a thick door that prevented me from going any further. I knocked once.

A grill slid open and a pair of eyes appeared from behind it.
"Password?"
"Barefoot waltz," I said.
The eyes behind the door disappeared. The sound of a heavy deadbolt sliding open indicated that the password was

correct. A moment later, the heavy door opened and a hand waved me through. I passed the big gorilla guarding the door without glancing at him.

As I entered through the large door of the dimly lit speakeasy, I was met by the sights of criminals, stumblebums, flappers, dirty cops, and just about everyone else who'd fallen on hard times after the stock market took a nosedive. They were gathered at narrow tables talking amongst themselves and enjoying all the food and drinks the bar had to offer. A band played Jazz music for the patrons of the crowded establishment on a small stage facing away from the door. A few people were shaking their legs on the dancefloor to the tune, but I ignored the music and scanned the large room for my contact; the same man who owned the joint.

I spotted him sitting in a booth on the far side of the room playing poker with another patron. He was an Arabic man whose real name meant "pleasant companion," but everyone around here just called him "Sam."

Sam wore a brown tailored suit and matching slacks. He had raven-black hair and welcoming brown eyes. For a man originally from Egypt, there was not a trace of his original accent whenever he spoke.

"Ha! I win!" The dark-skinned man exclaimed to the other man at the table and revealed the cards in his hand.

The unlucky man opposite him cursed angrily and threw his cards on the table.

As I approached, Sam spotted me and turned to the other man.

"Get lost," he said, "I'm tired of winning your money."

The other man began to sweep his pile of money back toward his side of the table. Sam noticed this and pointed his drawn pistol at the other player.

"Ah, ah, ah. Leave the money," he said, "You lost it fair and square."

Reluctantly, the other man walked away from the table empty-handed.

"Mind if I join you, Sam?"

"Of course, Guy," the dark-skinned man said, then gestured to an empty chair. "Have a seat."

Needing no further invitation, I occupied the chair across from him while he collected his winnings.

I tipped the brim of my still-soaked hat and let a small trickle of water drip onto the table next to Sam's winnings.

"Watch it!" Sam said, moving the money away before it got wet. "Jeez, can I get you a drink...or a towel?"

"Wouldn't mind a drink if you're buying," I said, "but first tell me something, Sam: anyone come by looking for me tonight?"

Sam placed the deck of cards in his trouser pocket.

"Yeah. There was a guy in here earlier, looking for you."

"Who? A client? A cop?"

"No. Just some big fella wearing a blue business suit. He's claiming to be a business associate of Capone. Haven't seen him in here before. He's over at the bar waiting for you."

I turned and glanced over at the bar. Sure enough, a tall, muscular man in a blue suit was standing by the bar flirting with a brunette dame. The man had a pencil-thin mustache and his oily hair was slicked back. I immediately recognized the man as, Marcus Wyant.

"He can wait a bit longer," I said. "What'd he want?"

"He didn't say. Only asked me to send you his way if you stopped in."

"Mhm..." I said, taking one last puff of my cigarette, before setting it in the ashtray. "I'll take that drink now if you're still buying."

"Sure," Sam waved the bartender over. "Hammett, bring Guy his usual. Put it on my tab."

A few minutes later, Hammett delivered a glass of bootleg whisky so strong, that it might as well have been poison and set it in front of me. I reached out, lifted the glass, and tilted my head back as the strong liquor ran down my throat.

I could tell by Sam's expression that he'd already caught a glimpse of the blood on my suit jacket. I quickly covered it with my coat.

"Your blood, or someone else's?"

I took another swig of my drink. "Couldn't tell you."

Sam looked over at Wyant, then back to me.

"You don't look so good, Guy? You in some kind of trouble?"

"Guess you could say that. I've had a hell of a day."

"What does one of Capone's goons want with you?"

"Old Scarface has some dirt on me he keeps holding over my head—even from behind bars. He's been using it to strongarm me into doing some small jobs for him on the side—Not by choice, mind you."

"Sounds like you made a deal with the Devil."

"You don't know the half of it. When Capone collects, he collects with interest."

I cradled the glass of hooch in my hands like it was a newborn's head and took another large gulp.

"What happened?"

"Let's just say, I got my hands dirtier than I would've liked during my last job for him."

"I'm going to need a bit more than that to go off of, Guy."

I let out a sigh. "Tell you what, Sam, you keep the drinks coming and my lips just might get a little looser."

Sam waved Hammett over again. The old bartender arrived with a tall bottle of the good stuff and began refilling my glass. I grabbed the bottle from him and placed it on the table.

"Leave the bottle," I said.

Reluctantly, the bartender walked away.

"That enough to loosen your lips?" Sam asked.

"For a while."

"Then why don't you start from the beginning?"

Chapter 2

A Phone Call and an Old Flame

It all started Tuesday night, while I was sitting in my office. It'd been a slow night. No new clients or cases to look into. I sat at my desk looking up at the spinning ceiling fan, which was doing nothing to keep the sweat from rolling down the back of my neck.

After losing my job as a detective to the corruption of this city, I'd spent the last two years setting up shop as a private eye. I'd had a couple of small jobs here and there, but nothing you'd read about in the papers—still, it was a good gig.

I sat back in my chair and lit a fresh cigarette. There was nothing else to do so I just watched the smoke blow about my office. It had been slow all day and I had even considered closing up for the night.

Suddenly, I heard the telephone bell ring in the other room. My secretary, Miss Kathrine Stevens, answered it. A moment later, she knocked on the office door.

"Come in," I said.

Kat Stevens turned the knob and stepped into my office. She was a beautiful young woman in her late twenties, with medium-length auburn hair that had tight curls and a pleasant romantic side part, which framed her delicate face. She had thick eyelashes and rose-red lipstick coated her lips. She wore a green Marcel Rochas suit with a matching skirt that stopped just above her ankles and a brand of perfume I couldn't quite place.

"There's a call from a Mr. Wyant on the other line for you."

"Thanks, doll. Send it through."

When the bell rang on the telephone, I answered immediately. If Marcus Wyant was calling me, it always meant trouble.

"This is Duncan."

The voice on the other end was far too familiar for a business call; the kind of familiar tone you'd expect from a distant acquaintance or salesperson pretending to be closer to you than they are. Wyant greeted me like an old buddy.

"Duncan! Glad I caught you. I'm not catching you at a bad time, am I?"

"If you were, would it matter?"

"No. It was just a formality."

I stroked my forehead.

"Cut to the chase, Wyant."

"I'm calling because our mutual business associate in the Cook County Jail has another job for you..."

I felt my stomach churn like it was trying to digest some rotten meat. I loathed calls from Capone's associates. Even locked away in prison, Al Capone was still running things with the help of his thugs.

"...Since he's been *away* these past few months, some of his competition's been trying to move in on his bootlegging business. He don't like people moving in on his turf. You remember what happened to Joe Aiello. He wants you to take out his competition for him."

"And if I say no?"

"A man like you's in no position to turn down a job like this. Be a real shame if something happened to that beautiful dame working in your office."

I scowled. That crossed the line. I could care less if Capone dragged my name through the mud again—hell, he'd already used whatever pull he had to get me kicked off the force a few years back. So my name was plenty dirty—but there was no way I was going to let Kat get caught up in my mess.

"I do this job and I'm square with your boss?"

"Sure. Sure. You'll be a free man. No more taking jobs for us or nothing after this. Just one last job and you're out. Promise."

I doubted he was telling the truth, but I didn't have any choice in the matter.

"Who am I looking for?" I asked with a sigh.

I could picture the ugly smile on Wyant's face.

"A small-time gangster from the south side named Alastor Nerezza has been trying to make a name for himself in the bootlegging business. Word on the street is he's doing pretty well for himself in his little operation.

"The boss wants him gone. You get what I'm saying?"

"I understand."

"I'm sure a private eye like you will have no trouble finding Nerezza and making sure he's taking a nice long dirt nap. We'll be keeping a close eye on you, so we'll know if you don't hold up your end of the bargain."

Without another word, he hung up.

And just like that, I was back in the mess, getting my hands dirty for Capone again. I'd gone from a disgraced-detective-turned-private-eye to a private-eye-moonlighting-as-a-button-man-for-Capone.

I quickly hung up the telephone, then reached over and opened my desk drawer. I removed an empty glass and the bottle of Listerine that I hid my booze in from it and poured myself a stiff drink.

It burned going down my throat, but I didn't care. It numbed the sewage line that my life had become. I loosened my tie and took another sip from the glass.

I heard the hallway door to the waiting area open. The frosted glass of my office door window made it difficult to see who had entered, but the silhouette was distinctly female. Whoever it was, was talking to Kat in the other room.

A moment later, Kat knocked on my door.

I quickly buttoned my collar and tightened my tie, then told her to "Come in."

Kat poked her head through the door:

"There's a Miss Desiree here to see you. She doesn't have an appointment though."

Desiree...Now, that was a name I'd never expected to hear again.

"Send her in," I said.

I sat up in my chair, as the other woman entered.

The first thing I noticed was her long slender gams. The rest of her soon passed through the door and into my office. She had round hips connected to a narrow waistline. Her neckline was impressive; it was sure to turn heads no matter what she wore. Her blonde hair was tucked under a tilted hat, but the hair that poked out emphasized her blue eyes.

She wore a black and white dress that would've been considered too formal to wear in the office, but not formal enough for a night on the town. In her left hand was a matching handbag of a similar style. The black heels covering her feet made her every movement seem sensual. You'd have to have been blind to not consider her beautiful.

For a dame I hadn't seen in ages, I tried not to let her charms get to me.

"Guy Duncan..." she said in a pleasant, yet seductive voice.

"Lola Desiree..." I answered.

She noticed the glass and bottle of "Listerine" on my desk.

"What're you drinking, handsome?"

"Mouthwash," I said, skirting the issue, then focused on uncovering the real reason for this unexpected visit. "You got a lot of nerve showing up here after what you did."

"I promise I wouldn't be here if it wasn't important."

"I'm sure."

She continued to stand in the doorway as if waiting for a formal invitation. When I didn't offer her a seat, she took the initiative.

"May I sit?"

"Might as well. I don't have any other clients lining up for my services at the moment."

Her round hips swayed with each step she took as she walked over to the chair opposite my desk and sat down. She pulled a cigarette from the container in her handbag and pressed it past her pouty lips.

As she fumbled around the contents of her handbag in search of her lighter, I quickly leaned over and offered her mine. She nodded her thanks and lit the end of the cigarette in her mouth. She took a deep breath, then puffed a cloud of smoke in my direction.

"Now," I said, sitting back in my chair, "why don't we cut the small talk and jump to the part where you tell me why you're here."

"All right. It's my sister, Lexi. I'm worried about her. I haven't heard from her in months. She doesn't call or visit anymore. It's just not like her."

I remembered Lexi. Last time I saw her, she was only nineteen—now she'd probably be twenty-one, maybe a little older. From what I remembered; she was almost the spitting image of her sister.

"She usually give you the silent treatment? Something happen recently between you two? Maybe an argument or a falling out of sorts?"

I saw Lola shift uncomfortably in her seat like she was sitting on an alligator ready to bite her in the butt. She looked around the office evasively but said nothing.

"Listen, toots, I let you in here out of professional courtesy, but if you're not going to be straight with me, then get up and walk back out that door. Don't waste my time."

I stood up and began to move towards the door; that loosened her lips.

"We...had an argument a few months back..."

I returned to my desk and sat down, while she continued:

"She'd been bitten by the love bug with some fella. Was head over heels for him, you see. She said it was love."

"Nothing out of the ordinary for a dame her age."

"She said she was going to run away with him. I-I may have lost my temper. I told her she was too young to be thinking that way. No matter how many times I tried to tell her that he was trouble, she wouldn't listen. I haven't seen her since."

There were tears welling up in those bright blue eyes of hers. She pulled a handkerchief out of her bag and dabbed at them, taking care not to smear her makeup.

"Why didn't you go to the cops with this sob story and file a missing person's report?"

"I did," she said, "They told me there's not much they can do since she walked away on her own and doesn't want to see me."

"I can't say I blame them. Truth is, if your sister doesn't want to see you, then that's her choice. You'll just have to live with that."

"You don't understand! The fella she's been seeing is working for some dangerous people!"

Her story was one violin short of a tragedy. Still, she'd piqued my interest.

"Dangerous people like who?"

"Nerezza...Alastor Nerezza."

Nerezza, I repeated in my head. If I played my cards right I'd kill two birds with one stone.

"Does this fella of hers have a name?"

She nodded. "Otis Agresta."

"Seems like an awful lot of players in this story of yours—which means trouble for me. Nerezza is one of Capone's competitors. I don't feel like getting caught up in a gang war all because your sister won't talk to you. You always did have a nasty habit of making choices that sent the people in your life packing."

There was fire behind those eyes of hers. I'd struck a nerve.

"Listen—I know I hurt you a while back, and you've got every reason not to help me, but Lexi's the only family I've got left in the world! She wasn't involved in what happened between us! Don't hold my choice against her!"

I looked past the angry front she was putting up and peered straight into her eyes—those damn blue eyes. There was some truth to what she was saying, and I knew it. With eyes like those, a dame could get away with more crimes than Al Capone ever could.

"Relax. I didn't say I wouldn't help you ..."

Her gaze softened.

"...but I ain't running a charity here. You want my help; you'll have to pay for it like everyone else."

She stood up, threw her arms around me, and planted a big one on my cheek before I had time to react.

"Thank you! Thank you!"

I pushed her off me. "Cut the funny business, toots. I'm not running a *Whoopee Service* here, so keep your arms and lips to yourself, understand?"

She blushed. "Sorry."

I straightened my tie and retreated behind my desk to put some small distance between us.

"I can't make any promises, but I'll see what I can do. I charge twenty-five dollars a day, plus expenses, and ask for the first payment up front."

Lola reached into her bag and paid in cash.

"When can you start?"

"I just did." I walked to the door. "I'll make a couple of calls and let you know what I hear. I take it you're still living at the same address?"

"Yes."

"Good. I'll be in touch."

I opened the door and showed Lola out. She turned in the doorway and looked back at me.

"It was nice seeing you again. Take care of yourself, Guy. Please be careful. If something happened to you—"

"Goodnight, Miss Desiree."

"Goodnight."

She walked out of my office, past Kat's desk, and out the front door.

Once Lola was through the door, Kat gave me an inquisitive look from behind her desk.

"I take it you've met her before?"

I shrugged. "A lifetime ago."

She raised an eyebrow as if she knew there was more to the story than what I was telling her.

"That's ancient history, Kat. She's just a client now. Nothing else."

"If you say so..."

Kat did not seem convinced. I detected a hint of jealousy.

I walked over to her and leaned against her desk.

"Besides—you know I only have eyes for you," I said, giving her a gentle kiss on the cheek, which was rewarded with a warm smile from her.

I glanced over at the clock on the wall: It was going on half-past-ten. I noticed the bags under Kat's eyes. It'd been a long day for the both of us. Unfortunately, I was in for a long night.

"Why don't you take the rest of the night off. I'll be working late tonight."

"Are you sure you don't want me to stay?"

"I'm sure. I need to make a couple of calls. You head home and get some shut-eye."

Kat started to gather her things. She put on her coat and lifted her handbag off the floor. As she got to her feet, she leaned in and kissed me on the cheek.

"Don't work too late. I'll be back in the morning."

I told her "good night" and watched her exit. The scent of her perfume still in my nostrils. Once she was gone, I walked back into my office and pulled the telephone closer, it was going to be a very long night.

CHAPTER 3

Cheese for a Rat

After I made a couple of calls, I agreed to meet with one of my usual stool-pigeons who said he had some information on Otis Agresta that he was willing to share.

As agreed, I met him at the corner of Randolph and Michigan around midnight – Not too far from where that reporter from the *Tribune,* Jake Lingle, had been killed last year for crossing the wrong people—*You remember the spot.* I arrived half an hour early to make sure I wasn't being double-crossed.

It was quiet; barely any cars on the street or anyone out for a nighttime stroll, so there weren't too many eyes looking in on my business there. I stood in the dimly lit shadow of the street corner and waited for my informant to show up with the latest rap he'd heard through the grapevine of the underworld. I trusted him as far as I could throw him, but most of the time his information was good.

He was right on time, as expected. Like me, he'd come alone. He had a short, unmuscular build to him, with a narrow face, and dirty-blond hair. The charcoal suit he wore looked one size too small on him, while the hat on his head looked one size too big.

"Well, Sid, I'm here like you asked. I've got a busy night ahead of me, so let's get this over with," I said, getting straight to business. "When we talked on the phone you mentioned that you had some information for me on Otis Agresta."

"Shhhh—Don't say his name too loud! Someone might hear!" he whispered, looking around nervously.

I looked around. There was no one around us.

"I don't have time for this, Sid. Either tell me what you know about Agresta, or I'm going to sock you in the jaw and leave you in the street for wasting my time."

"All right!" he said, holding his hands up in surrender. "All right! I'll tell you."

He looked around one more time before continuing:

"From what I've heard, Otis "the Fists" Agresta is trouble. He's been acting as muscle for one of Capone's rivals for a few months now. I'm told he beat a man within an inch of his life with his bare hands over a two-dollar dispute—then kept beating him! Haven't met him personally, but I ain't exactly itching to either. He's a wild one."

"Any chance he's been seen with a blonde dame, about twenty-one years old?"

Sid scratched his chin. "Come to think of it, I did hear something about that. Sounds like whenever she's around, is the only time he's on his best behavior. But when she ain't...it's best to steer clear of him. If I didn't know any better, I'd say he actually enjoys roughing folks up for his boss."

"His boss—You mean, Nerezza?"

Sid's face went pale.

"W-Where'd you hear that name?"

"I have my sources." Judging by the scared expression on his face, I could tell I was on the right track. "Is that who he's working for?"

The moment I mentioned Nerezza, Sid had gone from being the usual sly rat he was to a scared mouse. He looked around frantically as if saying the name would summon the devil it belonged to.

He lowered his voice, so even the shadows couldn't listen in on our conversation. "Agresta is Nerezza's right-hand man. He's the guy Nerezza sends after you when you messed up big time. When that happens, you may as well get yourself fitted for a *Chicago overcoat*, because you're as good as dead when he shows up."

"What can you tell me about Nerezza?" I asked, changing the focus of the conversation.

Sid shook his head like a stubborn child. This was more than he'd bargained for.

"Hey—Talking about Agresta's one thing—but ratting on Nerezza's like asking for a death sentence! I ain't messing with Nerezza! I told you about Agresta just like you wanted, so I'll take my money now!"

Fear has a way of shutting people up real quick. There are two ways to loosen the lips of a greedy snitch like Sid when that happens. I knew no amount of dough was going to get him to rat on Nerezza; so I had to go with my second option.

WACK!

I slapped Sid hard across the face. He didn't see it coming.

"You going to keep talking?"

"I-I—"

WACK!

"I don't have time for your bullshit, Sid! Talk!"

"All right!" Sid whimpered, quickly shielding his head before I could hit him again. "All right! I'll talk!"

I slowly lowered my hand, then reached into my jacket pocket. I casually put a new cigarette in my mouth and lit it.

Sid rubbed his sore cheek and let out a sigh.

"Outside the bootlegging business, Nerezza's been busy dealing under the table with some bad people. He's been slowly collecting whoever ain't backing Capone or Moran and putting them in his pocket. I'm talking button men, dope peddlers, weapon dealers, dirty johns, even a couple of highbinders—all on his payroll these days—though, he's not as well-connected as Capone or some of the other big names in this city.

"He's not the kind of guy you want to cross. I heard all the poor bastards that've tried taking him down have turned up dead. You don't even want to know what some of the stiffs that turned up looked like when he was through with them."

"Where can I find him?"

He looked at me like I was off my rocker.

"Why the hell would you want to go looking for him?"

He flinched when I raised my hand again.

"Okay!" He let out a defeated sigh. "Look—Word on the street is: Nerezza's throwing some big wingding—a masked ball or something—at the Drake Hotel tomorrow night for one of his big supporters. If he's going, I'm sure Agresta's bound to be there. That's all I know! Honest!"

Sid's scared eyes told me he was telling the truth. I reached inside the inner breast pocket of my jacket, pulled out a small stack of cash, and tossed it to Sid. He flipped through it greedily, then scurried away with his cheese.

I didn't return home that night. Instead, I made my way back to the office and put together a file on Otis and Nerezza. When I finished, I picked up the telephone and had the operator connect me with Lola's address. I poured myself a drink while I waited.

A sleepy voice answered a moment later: "Hello?"

Lola's angelic voice was in a dreamlike haze—somewhere on the cusp of awake and asleep. By the sound of it, she had been fast asleep when I called.

"Miss Desiree, it's Duncan. You stopped by my office with a job for me earlier this evening."

She yawned. "Yes. Yes. I remember."

I heard her stretch on the other end of the line. She sounded more awake.

"You don't need to be so formal, Guy. We've known each other long enough to be able to call me by my first name."

Under normal circumstances, it would've been easier to maintain some line of professionalism with a client—especially one of the opposite sex—but that damn voice of hers was as smooth as silk sheets and I was so exhausted that I found myself picturing her slender body lying across her bed. At that late hour, there was no use arguing with her.

"All right, Lola—" The name still didn't sit right on my tongue. "I apologize for calling you this late, but there're some new details regarding your case that I'd like to discuss with you first thing in the morning. Swing by the office any time after seven and I'll bring you up to speed."

She yawned again. "Sounds good, handsome. Goodnight."

I hung up the telephone and took another sip of my drink. Before I knew it, I was fast asleep. Soon, I was dreaming about a more intimate time with Lola...one that lived somewhere in the back of my memory.

CHAPTER 4

Envy's an Awful Shade

The next morning, I awoke to the sound of Kat calling my name from the other room. I heard my office door swing open and Kat's voice getting closer. I slowly lifted my head off my desk to see her standing in the doorway.

"Good heavens, Guy! Have you been here all night?"

I sat up in my chair. "I guess so. Must've dozed off while putting some files together for the Desiree Case."

A look of concern flashed across her face at the sight of the empty drinking glass and the dry bottle of hooch beside it on my desk. "I worry about you. Working all these late nights is beginning to take a toll on you. If you need to head home and rest—"

"I'm fine."

She did not look convinced.

"You're working later and later these nights, baby. I don't like it. You look like you barely got any sleep as it is."

"I'm fine."

She stepped behind my desk, wrapped her arms around me, and held me close. She was so close that I could smell the fruity perfume she was wearing on the nape of her neck. She kissed my temple.

"If you're not going to go home and sleep in your own bed, then the least you can do is come by my place and share mine tonight." She smiled coyly. "I'll make sure you get plenty of rest."

She slowly ran her fingers through my hair.

"It's been a while since you've done that," she said raising her brow.

It had been a while. Unfortunately, that would have to wait. I took her hand in mine and kissed it.

"I can't tonight, doll. I'll be following a lead for the Desiree Case."

"Oh..." Her gaze sank to the floor; the disappointment in it was as clear as day.

"I've got to chase this one before it goes cold. Don't know how long it'll take. Could be an hour, could be several. In any case, I can't expect you to be waiting up all night for me on the off chance I finish early."

Kat frowned. The look she gave me had the same effect as a kick in the gut. I didn't need eyes to tell that she was none too happy about me burning the midnight oil again.

If she only knew what I was trying to do for her. Honestly, there wasn't any way of telling her what I was doing for Capone without getting her swept up in my mess. So I kept it under wraps. The sooner I took care of Nerezza, the sooner I'd be free from Capone and his goons. Once that happened, there'd be plenty of time to make it up to her later.

"Things will be different once I finish the Desiree Case. I promise."

"I hope so...because I'm getting tired of trying to figure out where we stand these days."

Kat let go of me and quickly exited my office.

"Kathrine—"

Before I could say anything more, Lola Desiree opened the hallway door and stepped into the waiting room.

Kat waltzed past her without so much as giving her the time of day and sat down at her desk. I could tell she was still cross with me, but she wasn't going to let whatever was going on in her head keep her from helping me run the office. We were on the clock now.

"Mr. Duncan, Miss Desiree is here to see you," she said, with a hint of disdain.

"Thank you, Miss Stevens."

A moment later, Lola and I were alone in my office.

Lola wore a grey Empress Eugenie hat made of felt over her head that matched the wool dress she was wearing. It was far less fancy than the dress she'd worn the night before, but there was still an air of elegance about it.

I quickly threw my suit jacket over my shoulders and buttoned it up to make myself look more presentable.

"Thank you for coming, Miss Desiree."

"I told you: call me *Lola*."

I ignored the invitation.

"Why don't you take a seat, *Miss Desiree,* and quit bumping gums with me. I ain't got time for idle chatter."

She planted her rear in the chair across from my desk.

"Like I told you last night, I was able to dig up some information on Agresta and your sister."

The blonde's eyes widened nervously. "What kind of information? Is Lexi all right"

"Don't blow your wig. From what I've heard, your sister's safe. There's something else. Couldn't tell you over the phone—there're more than a few ears listening in on the switchboards these days—but there's a chance I may know where your sister's going to be tonight."

That perked Lola up. She scooted dangerously close to the edge of her seat.

"Really? Where?"

"I've reason to believe your sister will be at the Drake tonight with her man, Agresta, for some masked ball that his boss is throwing. I'm guessing her date is going to keep her close by while he's working, but from what I've been told, Lexi's been seen attending similar events with Agresta in the past.

"I was planning on dropping by and talking to her once she's alone. If I'm lucky, she'll remember me from the old days. Is there a message you want me to pass along to her?"

"If you're going tonight, then I'm coming too."

I shook my head. "I don't think that's a good idea. The last thing we need is an anxious broad jumping the gun and scaring her off."

"I'm going, Guy! Don't you try and stop me! Lexi's family—the only one I got left!"

Heavy tears ran down her cheeks, like rain gutters in a thunderstorm. It was an unflattering look on her. She turned away as if she couldn't bear to look at me.

"What happened to you, Guy? When did you get so cold?"

"Life happened. Eventually, I wised up and realized that I don't always get what I want. We can't all turn on the waterworks to get our way. Some of us get smacked in the kisser by the cold hard truth."

Lola looked back at me. Her lip quivered.

"If...If you're not going to help me, then I'll...I'll go myself."

She stood up and turned to leave.

I needed to stop her. The last thing I wanted was my client's picture turning up in the obituary. If she went alone and caused a scene at one of Nerezza's events, she'd be dead before morning. I couldn't let that happen—especially since she was the one paying me.

"Lo..."

She turned and looked at me before she reached the door. She seemed a bit surprised that I'd used her old nickname.

I had her attention again. By the looks of it, she'd be going whether or not I tried to talk her out of it. At least if I was taking her, I could keep an eye on her.

I let out a defeated sigh.

"You got something to wear tonight?"

She nodded.

"All right." I couldn't believe I was agreeing to it. "I'll swing by your place around eight. If you're not ready by then, I'll leave you behind. Understand?"

She nodded her head with much more excitement.

"It's a date." She headed back over to the door. "I have to get ready for tonight, Love! See you at eight!"

She blew a kiss in my direction as she exited my office.

"It's not a date!" I reminded her, but the blonde ignored me and walked further and further away until she was out the front door.

The rest of the day was nothing special. I went over my files on Agresta and Nerezza again and again. I had read their files so much that I could recite them in my sleep.

Before I knew it, it was starting to get dark.

After putting the files away in my desk drawer and locking it up, I walked over to Kat's desk. She was still busy typing up some papers.

"I'm going to take off for the night. I need to swing by my place and get cleaned up before I head over to an event at the Drake."

"With Miss Desiree?" Kat asked without looking up from the typewriter.

I knew where this was going. Normally, Kat wasn't the jealous type, but at that moment I could tell that she was none too happy with the idea of me spending time with Lola instead of her.

"It's just business. Nothing else."

She looked up at me and raised an eyebrow disapprovingly; clearly, her question had been answered. She stared at me in silence. I felt like she was interrogating me with her eyes. I didn't like it.

Another moment of silence passed. Kat was giving me nothing.

"Are you going to tell me what this is about, toots, or are you just going sit there gawking at me?"

She let out a frustrated sigh.

"I don't like Miss Desiree one bit. She looks like trouble. She's too friendly around you. I've seen how she's been looking at you since she first walked in here yesterday. Not to mention, you're spending an awful lot of time with her."

"There a law about spending too much time with a client while working a case?"

"Well, no—"

"Then quit jumping to the wrong conclusions. Envy's an awful shade of green on you, Kat. I said you got nothing to worry about, didn't I? So you got nothing to worry about.

"Lola and I are a closed file. I got no interest in digging up the past with her these days. The only relationship we have now is a business one. End of story."

I knew Kat wasn't going to let it go, but I didn't have the time to stick around and dance that dance with her that night. I had a job to do.

"I got places to be, so unless you got anything else you want to say to me, I'm going to get moving."

Before my hand could even turn the knob to leave, Kat stood up at her desk.

"Actually... There *is* something I've been meaning to talk to you about..."

I turned my head and shot her an annoyed look.

Kat's lip was trembling a little. At the time, I chalked it up to her being nervous and worked up about our previous conversation, but I thought nothing of it. For a second, she opened and closed her mouth like a fish out of water; fumbling for the words on the tip of her tongue, before finally giving up.

"...but I guess it can wait."

Before I was kept there any longer, I turned the knob and exited.

CHAPTER 5

3270 Memory Lane

At eight o'clock, on the dot, I pulled up in front of the apartment complex on 3270 North Pine Grove Avenue where Lola lived and parked on the street. The street may as well have been called *Memory Lane* because it was like stepping back into a past life. Not much had changed about the place. It was all as I remembered it.

I couldn't tell you how many times I'd visited this place back when Lola and I were an item, but it had been a few years since I'd last climbed the front steps to the lobby.

Nothing about the lobby had changed at all; The same potted plants were where they'd been before, somehow still clinging to life despite being overwatered and underwatered over the years. The same stained burgundy carpet was rolled out from the door to the front desk. I hardly ever remember a time when I'd seen it fully clean.

Just as I reached the front desk to have them ring upstairs, I heard the elevator doors open up.

"Looking for me, handsome?"

Out of the elevator stepped a blonde vision of beauty. Her stunning black-silk evening dress was a long backless one that hugged her voluptuous curves in just the right way and trailed across to the ground. It looked expensive; not what you'd expect to see a dame wearing in this part of town. Her hair had been done in a coiffure with several curls covering her dainty ears—she'd probably spend all day doing it to get it just right. There was a modest amount of blush and makeup on her face, with dark red lipstick coating her luscious lips. Her neck was decorated with her best jewelry that shimmered in the light like miniature stars.

I couldn't help but stare at her — I had eyes didn't I — It would've been a crime not to use them on that spectacle.

Lola did a little spin; the long skirt of her dress twirled with her.

"What do you think?"

In that light, the dress made her look—I shook myself from my momentary daze. She could dress in whatever glad rags she wanted, but it wouldn't change the dame wearing them. After all, a wolf in sheep's clothing is still a wolf.

I knew Lola well enough to recognize when she was fishing for a compliment. If I gave her one, it'd go straight to her head. I still didn't think letting her tag along was a good idea—but then again, when did I ever get what I wanted.

"Guy, I said, what do you think of my dress? Isn't it lovely?" she repeated.

I shrugged.

"Sure—Listen, Lola, this isn't a social call. I've got a job to do. The sooner we get a move on, the sooner I can get you out of my hair."

I led her to the car. We were on our way a short time later. She talked most of the ride. I just nodded my head and tuned her voice out. I was relieved when we finally pulled up to the Drake.

After stepping out of my black 1927 Model A Ford, and handing the keys to the valet, Lola and I put our masks over our faces and entered the hotel lobby.

The Drake always had a reputation for being a classy establishment, and that night was no exception. It was definitely an improvement from the dirty hole in the wall that I called an office. I can say this about the Drake: they love their chandeliers. The lobby ceiling was crawling with them.

While Lola was busy marveling at all that the lobby had to offer, I was scanning the crowds of people for someone matching the description Sid had given me. For an event run by a gangster, the guests sure knew how to clean up nicely. You'd have been forgiven for forgetting they were criminals.

Most of the masked guests were dressed in pristine black and white evening wear that most of the people living in the gutter would've been too poor to even dream about wearing. Looking around all I saw was a room full of rich pretentious snobs with deep pockets, liars, politicians—*the most famous liars of all*—and other criminals. I had no doubt most of the people there were the kind of scum of the earth who'd probably sell their own mother to further their selfish ambitions. Every one of them were trying to pass as model citizens—some were more convincing than others.

It was a world of black and white. In my experience, the world is rarely just black and white; it's grey. I make my living operating in the grey area. Even the most honest joe's got a couple of skeletons in his closet that he doesn't want the world to see. Everyone's got an angle, a line that they're willing to cross when times get tough. Anyone who tells you differently is conning you.

After comparing all the masked faces waiting in the lobby with the descriptions I'd been given, it was safe to say there was no sign of either Agresta or Lexi. I leaned in closer to Lola:

"I don't see your sister out here. I'm guessing she and Agresta are already inside. Come on, let's head in."

She nodded and followed me over to the large banquet hall connected to the lobby.

A group of Nerezza's goons were standing outside the hall and patting down all the guests before they could enter. When it was our turn to be searched, I noticed they were enjoying patting Lola down a bit too much. Despite our differences, I didn't like watching Lola being touched that way.

"You about done, pal?" I told the joker patting her down.

The goon removed his pudgy hands from Lola and shot me a dirty look. By the way he was handling her, you'd have thought it was his first time ever touching a dame. He shot me another dirty look before finishing up and nodded to the others.

"She's clean."

He waved me forward and instructed me to stretch my hands out before he started searching me. He was so close to me that I could smell the unappealing concoction of cheap cologne and cigar smoke that he'd decided to throw on himself that night. I felt him touch the model 1917 Savage pistol in the shoulder holster under my jacket. He held it in front of me.

"What's this?"

"What's it look like?"

"I mean, *why* you carrying it?"

"Occupational insurance."

The heavyset man tucked my gun in his belt and finished searching me. He turned to the others again:

"All right, he's clean." He pointed at me and gestured to my pistol in his belt. "You can get it back on your way out."

Before I could say anything more, I felt both of Lola's gloved arms curl around my left arm—You know the way a broad does when she's trying to be cute.

"Come on, Love. Let's head in."

I let out a sigh and walked into the banquet hall with Lola still attached to my arm. Lexi was there somewhere, but Nerezza and Agresta were the real people I wanted to see. Honestly, Lexi was just a means to an end—though I wasn't about to let Lola know that.

The banquet hall seemed to go on forever. Rows of pillars decorated with white and black ribbons stretched from one side of the hall to the other. There were tables for guests to sit at and a raised stage with a podium on the far end of the hall. That was where Nerezza would most likely be.

I looked around and my heart sank. It was so crowded that it was going to be next to impossible trying to find Lexi and Agresta in that mess of people. The fact that everyone—apart from hotel staff—was wearing masks did nothing but encourage the impossible.

Lola jumped up and down excitedly and pointed at a dance floor where a band was playing music for the guests itching to shake their legs on it.

"Oh look, a dance floor! What fun! You remember how to dance, don't you? I recall you asked me to go dancing on our first date. You were so good on your feet! Can we go...for old time's sake?"

She wasn't lying. I had asked her to go dancing before we started dating all those years ago. I also remembered that my feet were aching for weeks afterward. Unfortunately, I wasn't in the mood.

"I'm not here for dancing. I'm on the clock."

She pouted.

"Oh, you're no fun. When did you become such a stiff? The Guy I remember—"

"The Guy you remember died a long time ago when he caught you playing *patty cake* with his partner! Any feelings I had for you died that day. I'm here to do a job, not rekindle an old flame. Maybe this was a mistake."

I couldn't see the tears behind the black mask on her face, but they were there.

"I'm sorry!" she whimpered. "How many times do I have to say it? I made a mistake! But you were hardly ever around those last few weeks. A girl gets lonely after a while. I didn't want to hurt you. Honest."

I frowned. "Well, you got around to it anyway."

We stood there in silence. After a moment or so, she finally spoke:

"I can't do anything to take it back. I wish I could."

The previous song ended and the band played a slower one. It took me less than a second to recognize the tune of Hoagy Carmichael's *Stardust*—our song.

Fate has a bad habit of stirring up trouble where it doesn't belong—I'm beginning to think that Fate's probably a dame because only a dame would get a kick out of putting a fella in a position like that.

I hadn't heard that song in years. For a moment, I forgot the reason why we were there, as memory came flooding back like a wave in a hurricane: That first dance with Lola; The first time I held her in my arms as we swayed back and forth to the music—I remembered every detail of that night.

I shook myself out of my daze—I was slipping. I was there to find Agresta and then Nerezza. If I lost my head before then, I'd be a dead man. But the problem remained: I couldn't see Lexi or Agresta in the sea of masked people there. Little did I know a solution would present itself.

Lola looked over at the dance floor with the longing eyes of a schoolgirl, then turned her attention back to me.

"Just one dance... for old time's sake."

Those blue eyes of hers peered into mine like a siren's song, beckoning me to my demise. I had no chance of fighting it.

"One dance," I repeated succinctly.

I figured I'd have a better chance of spotting Lexi or Agresta from the dance floor than I would by just standing still.

Lola took me by the hand and led me to the heart of the dance floor. I put my hand on the base of her back, feeling the warmth of her skin against it. I felt her pulse quicken at my touch. Her breathing betrayed any front she was putting up to hide her excitement.

Once the oddity of dancing together wore off, she relaxed. During the song, she slowly inched herself closer to me until her head was resting on my shoulder—I'd be lying if I said a small part of me didn't miss that. For a brief moment—only a moment, mind you—I forgot all about Kat, Nerezza, and everyone else.

Like every moment of peace I've ever had, it was over too soon.

Out of the corner of my eye, a few feet from where we were dancing, I noticed another blonde minx with hair the same shade as Lola's. The girl was wearing a sightly white-silk dress that I was certain a dame her age wouldn't have been able to afford on her own—unless she had connections with someone rolling in dough.

Even with the white mask covering her eyes and nose, everything about this young broad matched Lexi's description.

My suspicions were further confirmed by the burly ape standing next to her.

"Come on, Odie! You promised me *at least* one dance."

The large, masked man accompanying her shook his head.

"You know I can't while I'm working, toots! Boss's orders."

I leaned in closer to Lola.

"I think I just spotted your sister," I whispered in her ear.

She slowly lifted her head. Using my head, I subtly gestured to where the pair was standing.

As soon as she laid eyes on the blonde, she nodded her head: It was Lexi.

I cautiously led her off the dance floor and toward where her sister and Agresta were talking. Neither of them noticed our approach. I could tell by the expression on Lexi's face that this was not the first time Agresta had broken a promise he'd made her.

She suddenly spotted us. I was sure she was going to rabbit. Instead, a smile broke across her face when she saw her sister.

"Lola!" Lexi said excitedly as she skipped over to her sister—not at all the kind of greeting you'd expect to receive from someone who's been trying to avoid you for months. She threw her arms around Lola. "It's so good to see you! I've missed you!"

Lola happily embraced her sister with open arms.

Agresta pushed his way forward. He stood at an impressive height of six feet. The muscles in his arms were so defined that it was a miracle the sleeves of his suit-jacket hadn't torn with each of his movements. Although he was dressed in a very dapper suit, he seemed underdressed compared to the other guests at the black-tie event. His dark black hair had been slicked back and almost matched the black mask covering his face.

The ground practically shook with each step he took. He certainly had the build of a *bruno*. Agresta looked like it would take half a police force to bring him down—and even then the chances were still in his favor.

He tore off his mask, tossed it aside, and stomped over to us. Agresta had the look of an overprotective swain; one willing to tell off anyone that came between him and his girl. His face was hard with a thick jawline. I noticed a slightly crooked beezer in the center of his wide face—likely from being broken repeatedly over the years. By the looks of him, I guessed he'd probably made a living as a boxer before Nerezza hired him. This man was clearly the man Sid had described to me, and then some. He stopped when he noticed Lola hugging Lexi. He squinted his grey-blue peepers and flared his nostrils the moment Lola came into view.

Lexi let go of her sister and turned back to Agresta.

"Otis, you remember my older sister, Lola."

He nodded while maintaining a look of distrust in the older dame's direction.

"I remember. Thought I told you to not bother us no more the last time I saw you."

Lexi gave him a slightly annoyed look.

"Oh relax, Odie. She's family. Don't be so mean." She turned back to Lola. "It's been ages since I've seen you. How'd you know I was going to be here of all places?"

Lola looked in my direction. "I had some help..."

I lifted my mask slightly to reveal my face.

"Is that—Is he—Guy?" I could tell she was trying to make sense of what she was seeing.

"Been a long time, kid."

Lexi quickly looked back and forth between her sister and me.

"Are the two of you—"

Before Lola could answer, I cut in. "No. Nothing like that. I was just helping her find you is all."

"Find me?" She looked genuinely confused. "She knew that I've been living with Odie for the past few months. I gave her the address and everything. She could've come to visit anytime."

I glanced over at Lola, who was glaring at Agresta. She lifted a finger and pointed it accusingly at the towering man.

"I would've, but every time I tried to visit, he'd just turn me away! What else was I supposed to do?"

It looked like things were going to get ugly. I stepped between the two of them before the fists started flying.

"Easy. Let's not lose our heads."

I don't care how much I was getting paid; I wasn't about to get my bell rung just because Lola didn't approve of her sister's taste in men. Agresta looked like he was just about ready to split her in half with his bare hands.

I quickly withdrew my cigarette case from my jacket pocket, and put the butt of one in my mouth, before offering one to the two-ton building standing in front of me.

"Cigarette?"

Agresta let out a low huff, but accepted my gesture, nevertheless. I lit the end of the cigarette in my mouth, then lit his. He took a deep breath and let a smokestack-sized cloud float toward the ceiling.

Once everyone had enough time to get their heads on straight, I glanced over at the stage where a group of politicians on Nerezza's payroll were gathered with their wives. Unfortunately, their benefactor was nowhere to be seen.

"Is our host going to make an appearance tonight?" I casually asked.

Agresta didn't answer.

I baited a little more.

"I hope so. I'd like to meet him, but I'm sure a businessman like him is far too busy to attend these events."

"He's here...but Mr. Nerezza's a very busy man. He doesn't have time to greet his guests personally."

"I understand. I hear he's got a lot on his plate these days."

Agresta grimaced. It seemed he wasn't as dim as most of the other goons Nerezza had hired. He knew when it was time to stop talking.

"I've got to get back to work. Excuse me." Without another word, he walked away.

I turned to Lexi, once he was out of view. "Is he always such a chatterbox?"

She shook her head. "Not when he's working. You'll have to excuse Odie. He's not usually like this. Honestly, he's very sweet when he wants to be."

"I'm sure." I lied—I've seen gorillas at the zoo with more manners than Agresta—but I was more interested in digging up more dirt on Nerezza than his hired goons. With her chaperone gone, now was the perfect time to see what Lexi knew about her man's boss. "I imagine his boss has been working him to the bone lately."

The shorter blonde jerked a nod. "Oh heavens yes! Odie has been coming home later and later each night. Most nights he's much too tired to even talk to me about his day. I worry that Mr. Nerezza may be working him too hard at the factory."

"The factory?"

"Yes. Odie's been putting in extra hours at Mr. Nerezza's factory so he can save up for our future. He's such a sweetheart. He always wants to make sure that I'm taken care of."

"Any idea what kind of products they're making at that factory—or where it's at?"

She shook her head. "He doesn't ever talk to me about it. I don't know where it even is. The only thing he says about it is that they've been under a lot of pressure to double their quota lately."

I could tell that Lexi had no idea what Agresta was really mixed-up in. I wouldn't get anything else out of her that I could use. It was time to look elsewhere.

I turned to leave. Before I could take a step, Lola grabbed my arm.

"Where are you going?"

"I'm leaving."

"Why?"

"The job's done. I found your sister for you. She's fine." Lola let go and allowed me to keep walking. "You can drop the final payment off in the morning with Miss Stevens in my office."

I could hear both dames trailing behind me. Without turning around, I told her:

"What're you following me for—I'm not giving you a kiss goodnight if that's what you're after?"

I stopped in my tracks.

Out of the corner of my eye, I spotted someone I could've gone the rest of my life without ever seeing again. A man I hadn't seen since my days working on the force. The first face in a long line of people responsible for flushing my life down the drain—I'd have killed for a stiff hooker of whiskey at that moment.

The last time I saw Detective Clive Hill, he was flat on his back, bleeding into the carpet of my apartment with a broken nose and more than a few bruises—Could've done much worse to him that night. I told myself if I ever saw his face again, he'd get a fist right in the kisser.

Hill flashed his shiny buzzer at the goons posted at the banquet hall entrance. To my surprise, they let him through—not one of them bothered to search him, let alone take the pistol that he was undoubtedly packing.

I felt the anger seething in my chest with each step he took. It was hard to believe there was ever a time we used to drink out of the same bottle.

"What's *he* doing here?"

"Who?" Lola followed my gaze and immediately spotted the man I was glaring at. She let out a sigh. "Oh, great..."

Lexi looked confused. "What? Who's that?"

"Detective Clive Hill. Guy had a falling out with him a few years ago."

"*A falling out?* I caught the two of you in my apartment together!" I countered in a low voice, so as not to draw attention to us. "I did what any sane person would've done after finding his partner *pitching woo* with his dame!"

"You pulled him off me and beat him to a pulp! You could've killed him!"

"Don't get dramatic."

"Me? *You* drew your pistol and fired a few shots at him while he tried to run! You're lucky Captain Allman only gave you a two-week suspension instead of locking you up for attempted murder!"

Lucky—That's not the word I would've used.

A few days after my suspension, one of the dirty cops in Capone's pocket told the chief that he suspected that I was selling secrets to Capone that he in turn was using to blackmail some of the other members of the force. None of it was true, but the planted evidence that turned up said differently. I lost everything that day; my badge, my gun, my job, my dame, and any sliver of trust I once had in humanity. I was a bum-cop with nothing to my name, except a shattered reputation. In the weeks that followed, I found I could see the corruption of the world a bit more clearly from the inside of a bottle.

I suddenly felt a growing thirst in my mouth.

"I need a drink," I muttered under my breath.

THE DEVIL YOU KNOW

I was so wrapped up in my thoughts that I hadn't seen the bastard approach us.

"Lola Desiree? Fancy seeing you here."

Lola turned around and came face to face with the detective. She smiled at the sight of him.

Hill was dressed in a light-grey suit that had been tailored to fit him and a matching fedora covering his head. His face was as clean-shaven as a schoolboy's — though with more mileage. There were deep stress lines on his forehead and between his brows, which made him look a few years older than he actually was. The bridge of his nose still showed faint signs of the previous break; I was glad I'd left something for him to remember me by.

He'd always been the kind of joe that the dames would pine after on long lonely nights. I'd heard it said on many occasions that if he hadn't found his calling in police work, he'd probably could have made a steady living working in the pictures. The more he smiled, the more I felt myself welcoming the urge to paste his pan with my fist, right across the jaw.

"Clive?" Lola answered, taken aback at his sudden appearance. "It's been too long. How are you?"

"I've been good." He shook his head in disbelief. "I almost didn't recognize you in that gorgeous mask and dress. You look breathtaking."

"You're not so bad yourself." She quickly gestured to her sister. "Oh, this is my sister, Lexi."

Hill smiled and introduced himself. "Detective Clive Hill. I work at the Detective Bureau. Might I say, you are just as beautiful as your sister?"

I rolled my eyes at his vagrant attempt at charm. As I turned to slip away, Hill recognized me immediately.

"My, my...Guy Duncan. Well, this is turning out to be quite the unexpected reunion," he said, as he looked me up and down. "You look...well."

I forced a smile. "Looks like your nose healed up nicely."

He ignored my crack at his appearance and carried on with the conversation. I could see all the small cogs in his head trying to work out the reason Lola and I were there together. For a skilled detective, he had a knack for jumping to the wrong conclusion.

"Looks like the two of you managed to patch things up since the last time we were all together. Frankly, I'm surprised Lola took you back, Guy."

Lola cut in before I managed to open my mouth:

"Oh, no. We're not together. Guy was just helping me find my sister." She gestured to Lexi

Hill looked confused but still tipped his hat to the younger blonde while keeping his focus on Lola. "Oh? I'm sorry. I saw you both together and thought—"

"Well, you thought wrong," I interrupted. "I'm seeing someone else these days. Get all the facts before you decide to close a case. I'm here on business. That's all."

He smirked as if he didn't fully believe me but continued to keep his thoughts to himself. I was losing my patience with him.

"I can tell by the bean-shooter you're packing under your jacket that you didn't come here for a social call. So tell me: What's a gum-shoe like you doing crashing a party like this?"

"Policework," he answered in a serious voice, then glanced at his wristwatch. "I wish I could stay and catch up, but I'm on the clock. Enjoy your night."

Once he walked away, Lola shot me a sour look. "That was rude. He was just saying hello."

"I'm surprised you didn't jump in his lap the moment you laid eyes on him."

"What's that supposed to mean?"

Lexi shifted uncomfortably, anxiously looking for an out before things got heated:

"Well...I should get back to the party. It was nice seeing you both. Have a good evening."

"Lexi, wait—" Lola protested, but Lexi had already disappeared into the crowd. "Great! Now she's gone!"

"So hire yourself another Shamus to track her down again. I'm done."

"I can't believe you!" she said in a huff. She stared at me with a stunned expression plastered on her face. Her gaze lingered for another moment before she finally turned and hurried after her sister, leaving me all by my lonesome.

I let her walk. Didn't have time for a dame cooking up half-truths, just so she had an excuse to see me. I'd been doing just fine without her.

As I turned to leave, I felt a burly hand on my shoulder and Agresta's low voice in my ear:

"Mr. Nerezza wants to see you in his office."

CHAPTER 6

Drinks with a Devil

I was led up a private stairway by Agresta and four of Nerezza's thugs. The other heavyset men were about a head taller than me, but none of them matched Otis in size or height. Everyone was quiet as we climbed the steps—you'd have thought I was being marched to my grave.

We arrived at a lonely door guarded by a tough-looking man about the same build as my other chaperones. There was a partially chewed toothpick wedged at the corner of his mouth in place of a cigarette. He nodded to Agresta and opened the door with a beefy hand that looked like it had sausages for fingers.

"He's expecting you..."

The thug behind me gave me a harsh shove through the door, then passed through it himself. The others followed suit.

I took in my new surroundings. The room was a fairly big one with a decent amount of space. On the far side of it, there was a large mahogany desk with a pair of leather chairs facing it. Several bookshelves were scattered along the walls of what could only be described as a private office of some kind. For a room with only a handful of lamps illuminating it, it was surprisingly well-lit.

My eyes were immediately drawn to a well-dressed man standing at the private bar with his back to us. His hair was neatly slicked back behind his head and his posture commanded a great deal of authority. He was definitely the high pillow of the operation.

Agresta approached the man and whispered something into his ear—I couldn't hear what he was saying, but he took his place behind me when he was finished.

"Otis, you can stay—the rest of you can clear out. I want to talk with our guest."

The four goons did as they were told, leaving the three of us alone in the office. The man poured himself a stiff drink from one of the glass decanters at the bar. Without turning, he said:

"Otis tells me you've been asking about me. Says you're eager to meet me. This true?"

"You could say that..." I answered.

"You a cop?"

"Not anymore."

He pointed to a leather chair facing the desk. "Take a seat."

I stayed standing.

"I said sit, or I'll have Otis help you to your seat. Capeesh?"

Reluctantly, I sat down in the chair—not that I had much say in the matter. Agresta stepped closer behind my chair in case I tried any funny business.

The other man finally turned around and took a sip of the contents in his glass.

"Ah..." he said, savoring the taste of his drink, "...Campbeltown Scotch, shipped in from Rieclachan,

Scotland. Those boys across the sea know how to make a damn-good whisky!"

Judging by the few grey hairs at his temples, the man was either in his late thirties or early forties; it was hard to tell. The mustache occupying the space between his honker and thin upper lip was pencil-thin and well-kept. There was a lit cigar in his mouth that glowed a deep red every time he inhaled it. His face was narrow with no visible scars on it. The grey eyes that rested behind his sockets were as icy as a winter storm and gave the clear impression that he had no patience for people who wasted his time.

He was dressed in a midnight-black satin dinner suit with a tall starch collar and jetted pockets that matched the tie around his neck. He had the look of a man who wasn't afraid to flex his power and wealth in public. There was no doubt that the man in front of me was Alastor Nerezza.

Nerezza stood behind his desk and puffed a cloud of smoke in my direction.

"I'm assuming you already know my name, so let me ask you yours."

"Duncan."

"Well, Mr. Duncan, have you been enjoying my party?"

I shrugged indifferently. "Hard to enjoy a party when you're as sober as a saint."

A small smile formed at the corner of Nerezza's mouth. "Ain't that the truth."

He walked back over to the bar and grabbed an empty glass from the counter, before reaching for one of the other decanters.

"Got the cure for that right here. What's your poison?"

"I'm fine."

He shook his head. "Nonsense! What kind of host would I be if I didn't offer you a drink?"

Before I could turn down his offer again, he was already pouring me a glass.

"Here—This'll put some hair on your chest. It's a new label called, McFinnigan's Irish Whiskey."

I eyed the glass suspiciously, held it up to my nose, and sniffed it; nothing but the usual wood aroma with a hint of vanilla that you'd expect from an Irish whiskey. The thirst I'd worked up over the course of the evening had finally won over my cautious mind. I tilted the glass back and took a small sip—I had to admit, it wasn't bad.

Nerezza sat down at his desk and grinned. "Not the usual watered-down stuff you're used to drinking at the local drum. It's good, isn't it?"

I nodded.

Nerezza casually leaned back in his seat and inhaled his cigar deeply. After holding it in his lungs for a moment, he let its thick cloud pass his lips as he released it. He leaned forward once again.

"So tell me this: Why's a man like you so interested in getting an audience with a man like me?"

"Word on the street is that you're trying to move in on the bootlegging business in the city now that Capone's gone," I said, taking a larger sip of my glass. "I hear you're doing well for yourself these days. Even have a factory you're using as a front to hide all the hooch you've been making and shipping out."

"How'd you find out what's going on at the docks?" Agresta demanded, butting in on the conversation.

The docks—I made a mental note to look into that later.

"I have my sources," I replied.

Agresta moved closer to pound the answers out of me, but his boss held up a hand. Nerezza's guard dog backed up at the gesture.

The older man smiled wickedly. "I'll admit, the bootlegging business has been much more profitable now that Old Scarface is in the hoosegow. Way I see it, that makes that empire of his ripe for the picking."

"Well, from what I've gathered, your name's been a popular topic in the underworld lately—though you're hardly in the same league as Bugs Moran. As impressive as your operation is, you're still behind Moran in the market."

Nerezza's smile faded. Didn't seem like he was too keen on me reminding him that he was second to Capone's competition. That ruffled his feathers. In turn, he shifted the focus of the conversation back on me.

"You still haven't told me what you're doing here."

"Working a job."

"What kinda job? Tailing innocent broads at late-night parties to earn a quick buck?"

I shrugged. "More or less." For my own health, I figured it best to leave out the part about being hired by Capone to kill him.

"You sound like a cop to me. I don't like cops. Ain't that right, Otis?"

I could feel the tower-of-muscle-behind-me, take a step closer to my chair. "That's right, boss."

"I ain't a cop."

"Sure you ain't..." Nerezza said sarcastically. "Funny thing is, Otis spotted you chatting with the dick that's been snooping around my party downstairs. You can see what a precarious position that puts you in. Who is he? Your partner? Spill it, before I have Otis loosen your lips."

I shook my head. "Just a dick who's caused me some trouble a while back. I broke his nose for it too. If you want to kill him, go right ahead. I won't stop you. You'd be doing me a solid."

He eyed me carefully, as if he was trying to read my thoughts, then smirked. The lethal sharpness in his grey eyes ease up a bit. For the moment, he seemed convinced.

"Like I told you before, I ain't a cop...and I sure as hell ain't a snitch for one—especially, that one."

"If you ain't a copper, then what are you?"

"A PI. No badge. Just ask those apes working the front door if they found one on me. They'll tell you—"

Out of nowhere, my head started spinning. I slowly felt myself beginning to nod off.

"That drink's stronger than I thought," I said, shaking myself awake.

The movement didn't seem to keep my eyes from drooping. It couldn't have been that late already.

I glanced at my watch: it wasn't even eleven yet.

The smile on Nerezza's face widened, taking on one far more nefarious than the one that he'd been wearing not too long ago.

"You should be more careful when drinking a good whiskey like that. I hear some of them will knock you flat on your ass," he said in a sinister tone.

I glanced over at the glass in front of me while I struggled to remain conscious. It didn't take too long to realize what had happened: the bastard had slipped me a Mickey Finn.

I clumsily brushed my glass over the edge of the desk as I reached out for Nerezza. My legs went numb before I could stand up.

Unable to make any defiant movements, I slumped back in the chair. I was fading fast. Darkness was creeping into the corners of my mind and filling my vision with it. There was nothing I could do about it.

I looked up at the blurring shape where Nerezza had been standing a moment ago.

"You going to kill me?" I slurred, as I lost feeling in everything but my noodle.

The darkening shape only chuckled:

"No. You'll live. Consider this a warning. Listen up and listen good, because I'm only going to tell you this once:

"I don't know who hired you for this job of yours, but if I ever catch you sticking your nose where it don't belong, you're a dead man. I hear you've been looking for me or asking around about my business; I'll have my boys pay you a little visit. I find out you've been meddling with my operation; I'll kill that tomato you brought here tonight and everyone else you care about before I finally knock you off too.

"You've got a lot to lose, so don't test me. It'll be the last mistake you ever make."

A moment later, everything went black.

CHAPTER 7

The First Good Sleep

I woke up alone in the driver's seat of my car with no memory of how I got there. What was more alarming was the fact that I was no longer at the Drake; somehow I'd managed to drive myself back to my apartment building while I was out. My head was still a bit groggy from the Mickey Finn that Nerezza slipped me.

After taking stock of myself, I determined I hadn't been injured during the trip. There was no way I would've been able to lug my unconscious behind all the way home myself. Someone must've driven the car home with me in it while I was out cold, then had someone else pick them up before I came to. The whole thing gave me a funny feeling.

I reached into my jacket for my pistol, only to find the holster empty. *Son of a Bitch!* I cursed to myself. *That goon never gave me back my pistol.* It wasn't like I didn't have others I could use, but they were up in my apartment or stashed away in my office. The office was too far, so if I wanted to get one of them I'd have to head upstairs.

That didn't seem like the safest choice at the moment. Someone drove me home, which meant they knew exactly where I lived. Who's to say that they weren't already upstairs waiting to jump me the moment I walked through the door. That wasn't a chance I was willing to take. I needed somewhere safe to stay the night.

The first place that came to mind was the office, but that was more than a hike on foot and I wasn't about to risk taking my car either—not to mention if Nerezza already knew where I lived, I was sure he already had that address too.

As my head cleared, I remembered Kat lived in a building less than a mile and a half from mine. I doubted Nerezza knew where she lived, so that was the safest place to be.

I exited my car and traveled in that direction on foot.

Once I reached Kat's building, I made my way up to the fifth floor and approached the door of apartment 537: Kat's place. I pounded on it loudly—No response.

I continued my relentless assault until I heard a familiar—and aggravated—voice on the other side of the door:

"I hear you! The *whole floor* hears you! You can quit it now! I'm coming!"

Her voice was followed by the sound of a series of locks and bolts being unlatched.

When the door finally opened, I was greeted with an eyeful of Kat Stevens dressed in a light satin robe that had been hastily tossed over the lacy peach-colored lingerie she'd been sleeping in—not that I hadn't seen any of it before.

Any makeup I'd seen decorating her face hours earlier had long since been removed. Even without it, she was still quite the looker. Locks of her auburn hair were disheveled and the tired-aggravated expression on her face was cause to believe she was prepared to club whoever had come between her and her beauty sleep.

"It's three in the morning. Some of us are trying to—" A look of surprise washed over her sleepy face; her aggression melted away when she saw me. "Oh, Guy. I'm sorry. I wasn't expecting you. Please come in and make yourself at home."

She quickly ushered me through the door and closed it behind me.

"Sorry about the late-night visit. Didn't wake you did I?"

"No. Not at all. I was already up." A long yawn escaped her lips and put a sizable hole through her flimsy lie. "Is everything all right?"

"No," I said bluntly, "I rubbed someone the wrong way while working the Desiree Case and opened a whole can of worms. I need a place to stay tonight. My apartment's being watched. I didn't know where else to go…"

I spent the next twenty or so minutes going over the night's events—while omitting certain details—and explained the pickle I found myself in. Kat listened intently as I brought her up to speed about the hornet's nest I'd just kicked. Not once did she try and interrupt me while I told my story—one of the many reasons that made her a damn-good secretary.

When I finished, she sat there and processed everything I'd dumped in her lap. I was half-expecting her to kick me out after hearing it all; to my surprise, she didn't.

"Well, that settles it…You're staying right here tonight. I'll throw an extra blanket on the bed for you."

"Don't trouble yourself, doll. I'll just crash on the floor."

She shook her head in protest. "Nonsense, baby! You're sleeping in my bed with me tonight. End of story. I still have that drawer full of the clothes you left behind the last time you spend the night. You'll be able to change before we head into the office tomorrow."

I couldn't keep my eyes off Kat. There was a sincereness in her bright blue eyes whenever she looked my way. Truthfully, I didn't deserve to have a dame as sweet as her taking care of me, but for some reason, she seemed to think so.

Without warning, I grabbed her by the robe and pulled her toward me so those luscious lips of hers pressed against mine.

She let out a *yelp* of surprise, but ultimately let herself melt completely into the kiss—even wrapped her arms behind my neck to pull herself closer.

For the first time in a long time, my heart was beating a mile a minute. Let me tell you, Sam, there's nothing like having a dame who's head over heels for you in your arms— especially one as beautiful as Kat.

Kat broke the kiss and led me by the hand to her bedroom. She stood beside her bed, giving me the most seductive look I'd ever seen. My clothes were in a pile on the floor before her robe even slid past her shoulders.

"My...Someone's excited," she said amused.

A moment later, she was lying across the bed—her goods on full display for my eager peepers. Her finger beckoned me to come closer.

"Well, don't just stand there, handsome. Come here."

I can't get into the details of what happened between us that night—but let me tell you, that was the first good sleep I'd had in a while.

When we finally made it into the office later that morning, Kat was practically glowing. The smile on her face reached from one ear to the other. Once the front door closed behind us, she threw her arms around me and planted a big one on my lips.

"I love you, Guy Duncan!" she said, with the same bedroom-eyes she'd been giving me all morning. I set my fedora on the desk beside her and started to loosen the clean tie I'd gotten from her place.

The thought of *making whoopie* with her on my desk crossed my mind—and it probably would've happened too if there hadn't been a knock on the door a moment later.

Knock! Knock!

I let out a disappointed groan and began to tighten my tie again.

"We'll have to pick this up later, toots," I whispered in her ear.

Knock! Knock!

Kat hopped off my desk, adjusted her skirt, then answered the door.

Lola Desiree walked through it, completely disregarding Kat, and made a beeline for my office. She did not look happy.

"Where have you been?" she demanded. "I've been trying to reach you all morning!"

I shook my head and placed my fedora over it again. Lola was the last person I wanted to deal with, let alone see.

"I got nothing to say to you, Lola. Like I told you last night: *the job's over*. I don't work for people who've been pulling the wool over my eyes from the start. It's bad for business."

The blonde looked offended.

"What're you talking about?"

"Don't play dumb with me. You knew exactly where your sister was the whole time. Don't deny it. I'm guessing you just needed an excuse to come crawling back through my door after all this time. Had nothing to do with Lexi at all."

She played the blameless card:

"I didn't lie. My sister *was* in danger. You saw how that thug treated her last night!"

"Save it!"

Lola looked desperate the more I unraveled her lie.

"So what if I didn't give you *all* the details. The truth is, I missed you, all right! How else was I supposed to get your attention?"

"Try sending a letter next time. It'll be easier for me to ignore. It could've saved you from wasting my time and your money. You want to keep dancing this same old dance—Well, my feet are getting sore—so I'm sitting it out and saving the next one for my new dancing partner."

I glanced over at Kat, then back to Lola, who looked confused.

"I can see you don't seem to grasp what I'm saying, so let me dumb it down for you: *I'm with someone else, toots.*"

The telephone rang.

Kat answered it in the other room, while I continued talking to Lola.

"The terms of our business relationship are over, Miss Desiree. You can leave your final payment with Miss Stevens over there on your way out."

A look of panic flashed over Lola's face. She was losing and she knew it.

"You can't stop looking now! My sister's still missing! I couldn't find her after she ran off again last night! She still hasn't come home yet!" she pleaded desperately.

"Not my problem."

"But—"

"Mr. Duncan," Kat called from the other room, "there's a *Detective Hill* on the line for you?"

I grimaced. *Another person* I didn't want to deal with.

"I'm not in," I lied.

"He says it's important. He told me he won't hang up until he talks to you."

I angrily picked up the telephone in my office and held the receiver to my ear.

"What do you want?"

"Well, *hello* to you too!" Hill said, on the other line.

"Talk, or I'm hanging up."

"I need you to come down to the station to answer a few questions."

"Like hell, I will."

"I'm afraid I must insist. I'd hate to have to send someone to bring you to the station the hard way. It's your choice."

He had me in a box—one I couldn't get out of unless I played ball with him.

"What's this about, Clive?"

"It's that Desiree-girl I saw you with last night. The one you were helping Lola find."

"Lexi?" I asked.

Lola perked up at the mention of her sister.

"What about her?" I continued.

"Her body turned up in an alleyway near Twenty-Second Street this morning. We haven't been able to reach Lola yet to break the news to her."

My eyes went back to Lola—the poor dame had no idea what was in store for her.

"She's here."

"Can I speak to her?"

I handed the horn over to Lola.

"Hello?... I'm good.... Did you find Lexi?..."

I watched as Hill broke the unfortunate news to her. I didn't need to hear the conversation to know when he dropped the bombshell—the moment she collapsed to her knees said it all. She sobbed something awful. Her makeup ran down as the tears poured from her eyes—I actually felt sorry for her.

Even for a bum like me, who had enough ice in his heart to sink the Titanic again—it was hard to see her like that.

CHAPTER 8

An Angel in the Morgue

After she collected herself enough to hang the Ameche back on the stand, I walked Lola to her car and drove it down to the Central Police Station on 11th and State Street, while Kat stayed behind. I didn't say anything the entire ride, in fear that the waterworks would start all over again if I opened my mouth.

When we arrived at the 13-story station, the pair of us were quickly led down to the morgue in the station's basement, where Detective Clive Hill was waiting for us.

There was a stiff on the metal table that was completely covered by a white sheet. There wasn't an overabundance of light in the room, other than the lights hanging from the ceiling. It was cold down there; the kind of cold you feel when you realize that sooner or later, we're all destined to wind up in a room just like it after we bite the big one. Doesn't matter who you are in this life, the undeniable truth is that death's the ultimate equalizer. No one can escape it in the end; not even Capone.

"Lola, I can't imagine what a challenging time this must be for you, but I need you to confirm the identity of the body for us," Hill said in a solemn voice.

The blonde dabbed the tears from her eyes with her handkerchief and nodded slowly.

Hill carefully removed the sheet covering the body. There was no denying it: *it was Lexi Desiree.*

I slowly removed my hat and lowered it out of respect for the dead girl.

Lola couldn't hold back her tears any longer. Lost in her despair, she flung herself into my arms and sobbed heavily once again. Not knowing what else to do, I let her weep into my chest.

As she wailed, I took in the vision of Lexi's cold lifeless body. The recently departed girl still retained her youthful looks; though her skin was paler than it was last night. Her pale skin in the light gave her still body an almost ethereal quality to it—like an angel from on high. You'd have been forgiven for thinking the young beauty was only sleeping—but the slug in the center of her forehead was a clear indication that Lexi Desiree would never again open those baby-blue eyes of hers.

She was still dressed in the white silk number she'd been wearing only hours ago. There were a few droplets of dried blood staining its front, but I'm sure the back of it was a dark crimson by now. Another thing I noticed was there were no rips or tears in it; which clearly indicated that there hadn't been a struggle.

Whoever killed poor Lexi wasn't a thief—I was able to arrive at that conclusion judging by the ice-studded jewelry still hanging from her ears and neck—they did it to send a message. As for the person pulling the strings, all signs pointed to Nerezza; that much I was certain of.

This had his stink all over it. It made sense. Lexi accidentally lets certain details slip and Nerezza sends someone to off her; the unoriginal way a mobster ties up loose ends. Still, I couldn't help but feel a sliver of pity for her getting caught up in all this. She deserved better.

Hill covered the dead girl's face with the sheet, while Lola cried her eyes out. I placed my lid over my head once the body was fully covered again.

"I'm sorry, Lo," he said, gently, with a hint of remorse in his voice. "Take a moment to say goodbye. When you're ready, Officer Peters will take you back upstairs and get you a nice cup of joe. He'll draw up the paperwork for the funeral arrangements. Please accept my deepest condolences."

Lola blew her nose into her soaked handkerchief. "Thank you" was all that she could manage before finally leaving the morgue.

As I turned to follow her, Hill held up a hand to stop me.

"Not you, Duncan. I got a couple of questions for you."

I followed the dick into a quiet holding room upstairs; the type of room a badge uses when he wants to put the screws on a criminal. I'd been in the room many times while I was still on the force with Hill, but I was normally the one asking the questions. I was all too familiar with the game Hill was playing; didn't mean I was going to play it with him.

Hill took a seat on the edge of the interrogation table and gestured for me to sit in the chair facing him.

"Pull up a chair, Guy."

I didn't move.

"I'll stand."

"Fine by me." He was playing the good cop; trying to get on my good side.

Like clockwork, Hill withdrew a pack of smokes from his jacket pocket and offered me one. I'd seen that trick coming a mile away.

"Cigarette?" he asked.

I shook my head.

"Then I'll cut to the chase; a girl's dead. The same girl I spotted you and Lola talking to just last night. Mind telling me what a cop—I'm sorry; ex-cop—like you was doing at an event hosted by a notorious criminal like Alastor Nerezza?"

"Heard the Drake makes a mean ham and cheese on rye."

The other man did not look amused. "Be serious."

"You already know. Lola told you herself last night."

"Ah, yes. She mentioned she hired you to find her sister. Is that correct?"

"More or less," I said.

Hill continued: "How'd you manage to find her, at a high-end event no less?"

"You're the dick. You should be able to figure it out."

"Humor me."

I sighed in frustration. "One of my sources tipped me off. Mentioned that a girl matching Lexi's description had been seen with one of Nerezza's thugs, Otis Agresta. They said Agresta's boss was throwing a party at the Drake. They figured since Agresta was working, the dame he was with would be there too."

"So you just...showed up. No invitation or anything?"

I shrugged. "No one asked to see one. Besides, I didn't have a shiny badge to flash around that lets me go wherever I please."

By the look on his face, I could tell Hill wanted to say something in response but elected to take the higher ground.

"We're getting off-topic," he said calmly. "At some point during the evening, you and Lola met up with Lexi. How'd that reunion play out?"

I crossed my arms.

"When we first approached Lexi, she was accompanied by Agresta."

"How would you describe their interaction with each other at the time?"

"Just a typical lover's quarrel. Nothing out of the ordinary. Seemed like Agresta had some beef with Lola—Something about her not approving of him being with her sister. He left soon after. That's about when you showed up."

"And after I left?"

"She gave us the breeze. Couldn't tell you where she went. All I know is that Lola went after her but lost her in the crowd."

"I'm surprised you didn't go with her."

I didn't say anything. The dick continued: "Getting back to Agresta; Any reason to believe he's the one that bumped her off?"

"No," I said, wagging my head, "From what I could tell, Agresta wasn't the kind of fella who liked sharing his girl with a crowd, but not the kind that would kill her for leaving a party without him."

Hill eased up a bit and shifted the discussion in a new direction.

"Let's talk about you. Where were you after Lola left?"

"What do you mean?"

"You must've gone somewhere when the girls left. So where'd you go?"

I could tell the direction Hill's questions were headed—and I didn't like it.

"Got pulled into a meeting I couldn't miss," I told him; I wasn't lying.

"A meeting with Nerezza?" he asked

Before I could answer, Hill interrupted me:

"Before you ask, I saw you heading to Nerezza's private office with a couple of thugs. Friends of yours?"

As usual, Hill had gotten his facts mixed up.

"Are you working for Nerezza?" he asked bluntly.

I kept my trap shut. There was no use arming him with ammunition he could use against me. Hill smiled and looked very proud of himself. He thought he held all the cards.

"I get it. You fall on hard times, so you end up turning to a gangster who'll throw a little dough your way in exchange for some favors. Does that sound about right?"

You have no idea how close he was to the truth. The only problem was he had his gangsters mixed up—but I wasn't about to tell him that.

"Admit it, Guy," he coaxed.

I kept my head.

"You looking for a confession? Try Old Saint Patrick's on West Adams Street. Otherwise, get your facts straight. I ain't working for Nerezza."

"Then mind telling me why he'd want you in his office?"

"He heard I'd been snooping around his party. Must've thought I was a cop, like you. When I straightened things out, he gave me a warning, then slipped me a *Mickey Finn*. Next thing I know, I'm waking up in my car outside my apartment with no idea how I got there."

Hill was busy jotting the facts down in his notebook as I set the record straight. He looked up from his notes.

"What time was that roughly?"

"Half-past-two."

He added the note with the others.

"One last question; Where were you between the hours of three and four?"

My alibi was as tight as a vault door. I knew exactly where I'd been between those hours and the hours that followed.

"My secretary's apartment." Hill raised an eyebrow. "Didn't think it was safe to head up to my place—given the circumstances."

"What were you doing there at such a late hour?"

I was getting tired of answering Hill's questions.

"The same thing most men do with a dame they've been seeing that's bound to tucker him out—I don't think I need to explain it to you. After we were done with *that*, we caught a bit of shut-eye."

Hill's face went red with embarrassment at my implication. He coughed his discomfort at the subject and cleared his throat. "...And she can verify that story?"

I nodded.

"That all?" I asked.

The detective finished scribbling a few lines in his notebook.

"For now," he said, "I know where to find you if I think of any more questions."

He took a quick glance at his notes, before continuing:

"Based on what you told me, it sounds like you were just in the wrong place at the wrong time. I would avoid any future *meetings* with the trouble boys in this city. People may start to think you're working for one." He gestured to the door. "In the meantime, I'm sure Lola is waiting for you."

I reached for the knob, only to be stopped by Hill again:

"Oh, and Guy..."

"Yeah?" I said, making little attempt to hide the annoyance in my voice.

"For what it's worth...when I heard the chief kicked you off the Force for dealing under the table with Capone—I never thought there was any truth to it."

I tipped my hat to him without a word, then headed out the door before he found an excuse to keep me there any longer.

Once I'd collected Lola, the two of us got in her car and made our way back to the office. During the drive, I wondered how many cops at the old station were in someone else's pocket; didn't matter whose pocket it was. The chances that there were more than a few dirty badges working that day were high. I couldn't point fingers at anyone specifically, but I knew they were there.

For all the beef I had with Hill, as far as cops went, he was one of the good ones—a bastard no doubt—but a good cop, nonetheless. Didn't mean I had to be all *buddy-buddy* with him. Either way, I wouldn't make the mistake of leaving him in a room alone with Kat.

I felt a delicate hand on my shoulder, which brought me back to reality.

Although she'd calmed down some, Lola was still a wreck. There were heavy bags under her eyes from all the crying. Gone was the fiery dame that had marched into my office this morning. In her place was a woman who looked like she'd lost everything.

"Promise...me..." she managed between sobs, "...Promise me...you'll find whoever killed Lexi...and...make them pay."

CHAPTER 9

Hard Facts and Simple Truths

"I'm telling you—Agresta's the one who killed my sister!"

Lola was on her feet angrily pacing around my office. She'd finally finished crying her eyes out, only to have us walking on eggshells. Her grief had quickly turned to rage. In her mind, Agresta was the only villain responsible for icing Lexi. I didn't share that narrow opinion. I looked at the facts and evidence—not emotion—before I started pointing fingers. The facts weren't adding up to the conclusion Lola wanted.

"You're letting that temper of yours blind you when you should be looking at the facts. I don't care if you like them," I said. "As hard as it may be for you to accept it, you can't change the fact that Lexi was in love with Agresta.

"He may have had a lousy way of showing it, but he cared for your sister in his way too. A little overprotective: *Yes*. He's no *John Gilbert*, I'll give you that, but from what I could tell, Agresta wouldn't have harmed a hair on your sister's head. In fact, I'm certain he'd kill anyone in this city *except* Lexi if given the choice.

"Besides, Agresta doesn't strike me as a triggerman. I'm told he prefers to beat his victims to death with his bare hands—you don't earn the nickname *Fists* using a gun. My guess is that Nerezza hired someone else to do it quietly, without his lapdog knowing."

"Who was it then?" Lola asked, after taking a moment to calm herself and process what I was telling her.

"No idea," I admitted, as I reached into the desk drawer and pulled out the folders I had on Nerezza and Agresta.

Lola raised a thin eyebrow at the folders on my desk.
"You already have folders on Otis and his boss?"

I nodded. "I don't like playing the game until I know who the players are. Better to keep tabs on the devils you know, than the ones you don't. I threw these files together with what I could dig up."

The blonde eyed the files eagerly. "Anything in there that'll help us."

"Maybe," I told her, while I flipped through my notes, "Last night, your sister mentioned something about a factory that Agresta was working at. Later, I overheard Agresta mention something about *the docks* to his boss—"

Lola's eyes widened. "You actually met Nerezza?"

"Wouldn't have called it a pleasant experience; but, yeah, I met him. He had his muscle pull me into his office after you left last night."

There was a genuine look of concern in her eyes. "Are you—"

"Look, sister, are you going to keep interrupting me, or can I talk now?" I snapped.

The blonde woman quickly took a seat in the chair opposite my desk. "Sorry. Continue."

"Like I was saying, I heard them talking about *the docks*. I'm willing to bet that's where Nerezza's set up his little bootlegging operation. If we find that factory, we find the man who killed your sister. I'll ask around and see what I can find.

"In the meantime, get yourself home and take it easy. You look like you could use some rest after the morning you've had."

It was true. The blonde had bags under her eyes that were big enough to carry a week's worth of dirty laundry to the cleaners. She looked like she was running on fumes.

"Maybe you're right," she admitted. "If you hear anything—"

"I know how to reach you."

The exhausted blonde made her way out of the office and paused in the doorway. Her eyes were on Kat, who was making subtle glances my way every now and then from behind her desk. It wasn't long before Lola put two and two together.

"Your secretary..." she said slowly, "...She's the one you were talking about last night. The one you're seeing."

I didn't offer a response. Didn't need to. She already knew the answer.

"Lucky girl," she said sadly.

I detected a hint of regret mixed with longing in her voice but ignored it. "Drive safe, Miss Desiree."

She took that as her cue to leave. Without another word, the blonde made her way through the next door and into the hallway.

Just then, the telephone rang. Kat picked it up.

"*Duncan PI*, how can I help you?... Yes.... He's here.... Who may I ask is calling?... One moment please...." She looked my way and covered the mouthpiece with her hand. "A Mr. Wyant wants to speak with you."

Not again, I thought to myself.

"Thanks, doll. I'll take it in my office."

I stepped back into my office and closed the door behind me. I picked up the handset a moment later and held the receiver to my ear.

"Talk fast, Wyant. I'm working."

"You know why I'm calling," Marcus Wyant said, in a far-less friendly tone than the one he'd used during his last call. "*He* heard about last night. Wanted to know why Nerezza's mug didn't turn up in the obituary this morning. He ain't happy about it neither."

"Something came up," I said, keeping the details to a minimum. "Tell him to keep his shirt on. I'll get it done."

"He better see some results soon or there'll be trouble. Maybe I'll pay that pretty secretary of yours a little visit to help motivate you—if you get what I'm saying."

The thought of Wyant putting his paws on Kat made me want to kill him all the more. Before I could say anything, Wyant added:

"You got two days to ice Nerezza, or you're a dead man. Capeesh?"

He hung up before I could give him my two cents.

"What do you mean 'two days'?... Hello! Hello!" I asked jiggling the switch a few times, but there was no response.

A heavy sigh escaped my lips as I sat down in my chair. After setting the phone back on the switch, I reached into my desk drawer for the bottle of *Listerine* I kept in it, only to find that I had polished it off the night before. There was nothing to satisfy the growing thirst in my mouth.

"Damn..." I said, staring at the empty bottle.

Two days. That didn't give me any time. I put my head in my hands.

Kat seemed to sense something was wrong. Without knocking, she stepped into my office.

"Baby, what's wrong?"

I couldn't begin to tell her.

"The Desiree Case is starting to get under your skin," I half-heard her say. She walked around my desk and rubbed my shoulders. "You should take it easy. You're going to work yourself to death if you keep this up."

Kat was right, but if I didn't get the job done for Capone I'd be a dead man anyway.

"I hate seeing you this way, baby," she frowned, "Is there anything I can do to help?"

I gently grabbed her hand and kissed the back of it once.

"No. Not right now." I faked a smile. "I'll be fine, doll. Just need to make a few calls."

The dame I didn't deserve smiled at me in a way that could chase storm clouds away. "Well, whatever's going on in that head of yours, I know you're going to get through it. You always do."

For both our sakes, I hoped she was right. Before exiting my office, Kat kissed my cheek. I breathed in the intoxicating scent of her perfume and sighed deeply. *What a dame.*

My eyes followed her as she passed through the door and returned to her desk in the other room. She was one of the few angels left in this city of devils. Compared to her, I was nothing more than a wicked sinner playing the saint. Maybe there was a road to redemption waiting for me once this job was done, but there would be no life with her unless I finished this last job for Capone.

It was time to stop daydreaming and get back to work. I picked up the horn again and wired several local speakeasies that I knew Sid frequented for information, in the hopes of tracking him down. Didn't have much luck with the first six, but I lucked out with the seventh.

With Sid's whereabouts in hand, I grabbed the extra pistol I kept stashed under my desk and placed it in my holster before I headed out; I wasn't about to be caught dead without one.

"Don't wait up, doll," I told Kat as I exited. "If anyone calls, tell them I'm not in the office."

CHAPTER 10

The Bee's Knees

A short time later, I made my way through a hidden door that led to a speakeasy called *the Hooch Hive* and began poking around for Sid. I didn't have to look too hard to find him. It was still early in the day, so the usual crowd was not occupying the place like it would be later that night. There wasn't even any music playing or any other kind of entertainment, just a handful of drunks who'd worked up an early thirst before the place got jumping.

Compared to *the Drifter*, the Hive wasn't much to bat an eye at, but it still managed to bring in a crowd for its nightlife. There were several tables scattered around the place, with a few stools at the bar. The small stage, which was usually lit for the band, was dark and empty. Apparently, I'd beat the rush.

I spotted Sid sitting at one of the tables with two roundheels on the ends of his arms, and a tall bottle of bathtub gin on the table in front of him. Both dames were easy on the eyes, but I was sure they were only putting on a show for him as long as he kept their pockets fed with plenty of lettuce—they probably would have done the same for a troll, if he was paying them enough. Sid didn't seem to mind one way or another.

THE DEVIL YOU KNOW

He poured them each another drink until the bottle was empty.

"What did you say this drink was called again?" the blonde on his right asked, slightly slurring her words.

"*The Bee's Knees*," he answered with a smile, then took another swig of his drink, "...Ain't it just?"

The brunette on his left was the first to notice my approach. "Who's your friend?"

Sid almost choked on his drink when he saw me.

"Duncan—I didn't know you was coming."

"Figured I'd find you in a joint like this," I said.

"What's wrong with a place like this? I got a roof over my head, some green in my pocket, a drink in my hand, and two beautiful tomatoes sitting beside me. It's the bee's knees." He pulled the girls in closer and downed his glass in one gulp.

I hadn't come there for pleasure. "Lose the dames. I want to talk with you..."

The broads didn't move.

"...*alone*," I added.

The rat looked disappointed but reluctantly agreed.

"All right, girls. You heard him. Scram. I've got to talk business."

Both dames stood up and walked away from the table, in search of another easy mark to sucker into buying them a drink.

Sid looked back at me. "Well, seeing as you chased away my dates, I think you owe me a drink."

I waved the bartender over.

"Two of whatever he's drinking—and make mine a double."

The bartender went to fetch our drinks, leaving us alone.

Sid sat back in his chair and crossed his arms. "What's the occasion for this little visit?"

"I need information."

A greedy smile broke across his lips. He leaned forward and rubbed his mitts together.

"I got the scoop if you got the dough."

"You'll get it after I get the information."

"Working a new case or something?" he pried.

"Or something," I answered.

Sid made a living off of selling people's secrets. What was stopping him from selling mine too? The less information I supplied him with, the less he had to gain.

"You know anything about a bootlegging operation happening down by the docks?"

"We talking shipping or production?"

"Production—but could be both. It would be in a smaller factory."

Sid's eyes filled with fear. He knew exactly what place I was talking about, and who was running it.

"You're still looking into...*You-Know-Who*?"

I nodded. The answer did nothing to calm his nerves.

"I-I can't help you..." he said with a nervous quiver in his voice, "I'm lucky none of his thugs came knocking on my door for giving you the information you got out of me the other night."

"Then you know *exactly* where the factory is."

"Of course, I know where it is! Doesn't mean I'm willing to paint a target on my melon for telling you about it!"

Sid looked like he was about to bolt—the only problem was that I was the one thing standing between him and the door. He made a clumsy attempt for the exit, but the amount of gin running through his veins only unbalanced his footing. A second later, he tripped and was on the ground before I set a finger on him.

I lifted him off the floor and helped him back into his chair, then sat beside him.

"You finished making any more dumb discissions?" I asked.

The tipsy rat nodded.

"Good. Now, you're going to tell me everything you know about Nerezza's operation down at the docks, or I'm going to smack your ugly mug until it's so nasty, that even the pro skirts in this town won't want to be seen with you, no matter how much dough you throw their way."

The mix of sobering terror and understanding in Sid's eyes gave me reason to believe that he wasn't dumb enough to try and run a second time.

The bartender returned with our drinks and placed them on the table. I slipped him a century before he walked away. The rat grabbed his glass and cradled it like an infant with a bottle.

I took a sip of my drink. "Now, start talking. You can start by telling me *where* Nerezza's factory is."

Sid lifted the glass in his trembling hands toward his lips and took a generous gulp. "I-I can't."

I was losing my patience with the coward. I grabbed him by his left ear and gave it a good tug. He winced in pain.

"You listening, Sid?" I said sternly, "I asked you a question! Where is the factory Nerezza's been operating out of?"

There was still a sliver of defiance left in his frightened eyes—I had to admit, I was impressed that he hadn't cracked already. So I tugged harder. He cried out in pain.

"Last chance, Sid! Talk!"

He finally caved. "All Right! It's on the edge of the city—in the old soup factory—down by the lake! It's the truth! I swear!"

I let go of his ear. "See. Was that so hard?"

Sid eyed me with a look of disdain. I ignored it. I didn't care if he hated me or not, the only thing I was after was the information.

"Nerezza there often?"

The other man rubbed his ear and nodded.

"Sure. Every once in a while. But he has his goons overseeing most of the work, making sure all the workers stay in line—you know how it is. I heard from a buddy of mine that they work you to the bone, then keep working you. He told me if you start slowing down, or can't work no more, one of the brunos will persuade you into getting back to work. If that don't do the trick — well, let's just say it ain't pretty.

"From what I heard, the two big ones running things while Nerezza's away are Agresta and Bernie 'Ashes' Burns."

I knew all about Ashes Burns from my time as a cop. He had a laundry list of crimes to his name a mile long; arson, property damage, armed robbery, battery, assault, and murder, to name a few off the top of my head. Regardless of what he was wanted for, he was a dangerous one.

If Nerezza had Burns and Agresta working for him, there was bound to be trouble.

"I'm guessing there's more than a couple of gunsels guarding the place?" I figured.

Sid nodded. "Plenty! I'm telling you, it's not the kind of place you visit unless you've got a death wish! Best to steer clear of that joint altogether!"

He was fidgeting in his seat with fear.

"Look, I told you what you wanted to know. Now pay up."

I calmly finished my drink and wiped my mouth with my sleeve. "You'll get your money. But first, you and I are going to take a little ride in your car—and you're going to take me to the factory."

Sid looked confused. "Wait—Take you there? That wasn't part of the deal."

"Well, the way I see it, the moment I walk out of this drum, you'll most likely do something stupid, like tip Nerezza off to the fact that I'm coming and earn yourself some extra dough for double-crossing me. They find out and wait for me to walk right into the trap."

The rat was sweating more than a wet sponge. "I would never!"

I knew Sid better than that. He'd have sold his own mother to the Devil himself if it put a little more dough in his pocket.

"Save it. I ain't in the mood. Tonight, you're going to drive me *exactly* where I want to go."

"But...But he'll kill me!"

I made sure Sid heard the *Click* of my pistol, which was aimed directly at his gut from under the table.

"I'll kill you sooner if you don't take me. I just won't enjoy it as much as Nerezza will."

That made Sid reevaluate his options. "Fine. I'll do it—But I want my money upfront!"

"Fine by me," I said, setting a couple of C's on the table with my free hand. "Don't spend it all in one place...or on one broad."

The rat greedily collected his cheese; the prospect of death seemed to, for the moment, have slipped his mind. He flipped through the stacks of bills, making sure all of it was there.

"Let's just get this over with," he sighed, before downing the rest of his drink.

Sid was one more drink away from going over the edge with the rams. He needed time to sober up before we went anywhere. Besides, it was still light out. Going now would get us both killed.

I shook my head. "Not now. We'll wait until tonight when it's dark. That should give you time to sober up."

"You're funeral."

I waved the bartender over again. "He'll take a cup of joe. Black. Keep them coming."

The bartender returned a moment later with the steaming beverage.

Sid looked down at the black drink with disgust.

"Great. I was hoping I wouldn't have to do this sober," I heard him mumble under his breath.

CHAPTER 11

The Gin Mill and a Couple of Chasers

We arrived at the old factory in the dead of night, under the cover of darkness. Sid parked the car a safe distance away from it, taking care to keep it out of view.

"This is the place," he said, "just like I told you."

I looked out at the old factory. The building itself had seen better days since the stock market crashed two years ago; a few chunks of brickwork had crumbled away here and there, but the overall factory was in good shape. It was the ideal size for an operation someone wanted to keep off the books; big enough to house all the equipment, but small enough to not draw attention.

As far as the city knew, it was just a small factory down by the docks, the same as any other. Using Lake Michigan, Nerezza's goons could easily slip shipments in and out of the city by boat, or off to any of the three neighboring states that bordered its waters.

"Well, pleasure doing business with you. I'll just let you out here and be on my—"

I cut Sid off before he could weasel himself out of the situation.

"Nice try," I said, pointing my pistol at him. "Get out. You're coming too."

I lowered my pistol so it was aimed just below his beltline.

"You try to run, or attempt to draw any attention to us—you'll be singing soprano 'til the end of your days. Understand?"

Sid nodded nervously as he exited the driver-side door. I exited from the passenger side soon after; my pistol never moving from its target. We slowly began our approach.

As we got closer on foot, using the large stacks of wooden crates as cover, I noticed an open door on the southeast side of the building. I motioned for Sid to head in that direction—he wasn't happy about it, but he made his way to it, while I followed closely behind.

Surprisingly, there was no one guarding it. I cautiously poked my head around the corner to get a better look inside. After deciding it was safe, I gestured for Sid to head in first.

We passed a series of oak barrels stacked up high along the wall as we continued forward. Thankfully, there were plenty of shadows to duck in and out of as we went.

At the end of the long hallway, I heard the sound of raised voices echoing off the walls. It was coming from deeper in the factory. It sounded like a fistfight had erupted—which explained why the guards weren't at their posts. The voices grew louder and louder as more voices joined in and attempted to calm the situation:

"Fists, knock it off! He didn't mean it! It was just a joke!"
"He's going to kill him with a beating like that!"

As we followed the voices, I spotted four thugs standing near a series of much larger oak barrels in the cellar. They were struggling to restrain a tall muscular man, who I immediately recognized as Agresta. Their efforts did little to slow him down, as he continued using his bloodied fists to play chin music on the unfortunate bastard sprawled out on the floor.

The savage assault did not let up either. Agresta was a man off his track. He was lost in the animalistic violence his fists were creating.

Another man had his hand on Agresta's shoulder, despite being a foot or so shorter than the towering man.

"Take it easy, Fists..."

Agresta slowly began to calm down; though, I was sure the man on the receiving end of those fists, was already dead.

"...Vinnie didn't mean nothing by it."

The man glanced down at the bloody body on the floor.

"Christ..." he said under his breath, then waved one of the other thugs over. "Get this mess cleaned up before the boss gets back."

He looked up at the other workers, who were standing dumbfounded by the whole ordeal. "The rest of you, get back to work! Those vats better not boil over 'cause you were slacking off!"

The workers quickly scurried back to their stations and resumed their tasks.

I caught a better glimpse of the man barking the orders once he stepped into the light.

The first thing I noticed was the burns on the left side of his face. The burnt skin was red and slightly charred—probably from a recent accident in the factory. There were some patches of hair missing from the side of his head, with some burn scars near his left temple.

Despite his scarred appearance, the man was dressed in a neatly tailored Pinstripe suit and tie that gave him an impression of authority over the factory.

Sid pointed at the man and whispered: "That's Ashes Burns!"

Burns turned back to Agresta and placed his hand back on the man's shoulder.

"I get you're all broken up about your dame turning up dead this morning, but you can't just slug a guy for cracking a joke to lighten the mood. We can't start turning on our own. It's bad for business."

Until then, I failed to notice that Agresta had multiple rips and tears in the seams of the sleeves and the shoulders of his jacket, but he was otherwise unharmed. He was still huffing with raw emotion.

"If I ever get my hands on whoever killed my Lexi, I'm going to beat them bloody until there's nothing left! Their own mother won't be able to recognize them!"

This confirmed my suspicions; Agresta hadn't killed Lexi, someone else had—and by the sound of it, he wasn't sure who did it either.

Burns shook his head:

"I'm right there with you, Fists, but we got a job to do here. We can't get it done if you keep losing it. Listen — you've had a hell of a day. Head home. Get your head on straight. I'll take care of things here and make sure the hooch gets shipped out tonight.

"The boss needs you sharp when you come in tomorrow morning. Don't go getting soft on him now."

Sid and I followed the two thugs, cautiously keeping our distance in the shadows. Burns led Agresta to a car parked out front. The towering body of raw emotion and muscle entered it a moment later and drove away.

When the car was out of view, Burns turned to one of the other thugs.

"He's gotten softer since he started seeing that dame of his. Now that she's gone, I'm sure he'll be back to the ruthless son of a bitch he was in no time," he said. "All right. Have the boys start loading the crates. The boss wants to keep the next shipment on schedule."

"He coming tonight?" the other man asked.

"Doubt it, but if we don't get these shipments out, there will be hell to pay."

I turned back to Sid.

"Sounds like Nerezza's not coming," I said in a low voice. "I've heard all I needed to hear tonight."

A look of relief washed over Sid's face.

"About time! I told you this place was trouble. We're lucky Burns didn't spot us." He slowly began to back up. "Maybe we can still make it out of here alive. We just need to be—"

Sid's back bumped into a crate with empty bottles on top of it. The bottles came crashing to the floor loudly.

"Hey-What was that?" one of the goons shouted. "It came from over there!"

Burns immediately spotted us. "There they are! Pump them full of lead!"

The two of us sprinted down the hallway as the bullets started flying; a few of them poked holes in the stacked barrels, causing them to leak their contents onto the floor. A round of more bullets joined in.

By some miracle, we made it outside and booked it to the car with a trail of bullets hot on our heels.

The mob of goons quickly poured out of the factory and continued shooting at us.

Sid opened the car door with shaking hands. "We're in it now! They're going to kill us!"

"Shut up and drive!" I yelled, piling into the car.

A moment later, we were speeding away.

In the distance, I heard Burns ordering his hatchetmen to "Pull the cars around," so they could follow us. He was not about to let us get away without a fight.

"Did we lose them?" Sid asked frantically.

I spotted three cars tailing us in the rearview mirror.

Their engines roared as they raced after us.

"Not yet," I answered.

The thugs' cars were getting closer.

We quickly turned onto the main road and drove back into the city, hoping to lose the other cars. Sid swerved between the cars in front of us like a madman. I had to brace myself when he turned sharply onto another street.

Despite the wild maneuvers, Burns and his men were still in hot pursuit.

A round of bullets passed through the rear window of Sid's car; we had to duck our heads down to avoid being hit. I looked back and saw three gunmen packing Thompsons from the passenger-side windows, while they pressed their bodies against the roofs of their speeding cars for balance and continued to squirt metal in our direction.

"Now they're shooting at us!" Sid shouted. "We're dead. We're dead."

"Shut up and keep driving!"

I raised my gun and returned fire through the back window. One of my bullets struck the goon driving the car on the right, square in the throat.

The driver, grabbed at his punctured windpipe as his car swerved into the other lane of oncoming traffic and crashed into several of the approaching cars.

"Make a hard left here!" I ordered. Sid did as he was told.

Our tires screeched from the sharp maneuver, turning the car onto the next street. Horns of civilian cars honked loudly, while their drivers slammed on their breaks to avoid a collision.

The lead car followed us without a hitch, but its escort collided with two civilian cars when it attempted to follow; its gunner was thrown from the driver-side window and onto the street where he was immediately trampled to death by a wave of cars.

It was just us and the lead car.

A searing pain shot through my left arm after a stray bullet passed through it—thankfully missing the bone. I lifted my pistol and shot the gunner before he could reload his weapon.

The goon's body hung as lifelessly as a ragdoll from the window.

Burns climbed over the backseat and pushed the rest of the dead weight out of the car, then continued firing at us with his drawn pistol.

"Get alongside them!" I heard him shout to his driver.

With a sudden roar of the engine, the car was right beside us. Burns fired his pistol at me several times, missing me by a fraction of an inch.

Suddenly, our car swerved out of control and collided with a large brick wall. I got my bell rung pretty hard from the impact. The taste of blood filled my mouth. I was sure my nose was broken and there was a cut on my forehead, along with a few minor scratches.

I looked at the nose of Sid's car: it was in bad shape. The whole hood had been flattened and one of the front wheels had been bent uselessly on the sidewalk. There was no way it was going anywhere anytime soon.

"What the hell was that?" I cursed. "You let them run us off the road! What were you—"

I stopped in mid-sentence once I looked over in Sid's direction; his head was lying against the steering wheel.

"Sid?" I asked, again and again, hoping to get a response while I assessed his injuries.

My heart sank. In addition to a broken neck—no doubt, a result of the impact—Sid had a bad case of lead poisoning. I noticed several entry wounds in his left temple; he'd been dead before his car even hit the wall.

I quickly picked my ruffled hat off the pavement, placed it back on my head, and reloaded my pistol. Afterward, I reached into my jacket pocket and lit a cigarette for myself.

As I reached across the seat to retrieve Sid's body, the sound of tires turning on the hard asphalt echoed through the street. Burns was turning around to finish us off. I didn't have time to get to the body before Burns' car came into view from the other end of the street.

His headlights were aimed directly at Sid's wreck and approaching fast. I fought through the pain coursing through my body and fired the whole round at the gangster's car.

At the last minute, the car turned and collided with Sid's. It jumped the curb and flipped upside down. I noticed the driver was dead with a bullet hole through his forehead.

The smell of gasoline filled the air. A sizeable puddle of it had collected between the two cars.

From where I was standing, I had a clear view of Ashes Burns as he attempted to crawl out of his car. Both his legs were broken and his bell had been rung much harder than mine. The crimson trickled down his face from the open gash across his head. He managed to roll through the shattered window and into the puddle of gasoline.

Just as he attempted to raise his pistol, I tossed my lighter between the two cars. The flammable liquid caught fire, engulfing the space in an instant. Burns screamed as his broken body was consumed by the flames.

Soon, the screaming stopped altogether and the sound of sirens could be heard approaching from the distance. They were still a ways off. It would be some time before they managed to get through all the wreckage the chase had left behind.

Not wanting to find myself in Hill's office a second time, I slowly limped away from the scene and headed back to my apartment through every back alleyway I could think of.

CHAPTER 12

Secrets and Seduction

Shortly after returning home, I stumbled through the door of my apartment and immediately staggered over to the bookshelf in my study, where I hid a few bottles of absinthe. I popped off the cork of the first bottle and took a quick swig to numb the pain wracking my body. I didn't even feel the burn of the alcohol as it traveled down my throat.

Once the *medicine* kicked in and the pain had lessened substantially, I limped over to the bathroom to start patching myself up. I quickly tied one of my spare towels around my wounded arm and used it to stop the bleeding. Then, I stitched myself up with the sewing kit I kept in the drawer, before finally snapping my nose back into place—-that hurt like an empty bottle of hooch.

After I'd shucked off my soiled clothes and tossed them in the hamper, I poured myself another stiff drink. When I was somewhere between *smoked* and *tipsy*, I decided to retire to the bedroom to get some shut-eye.

As I pulled back the covers and rested my head against the pillow, I felt a dainty hand dance across my chest. Not knowing who the said hand belonged to, I quickly—as quickly as my injured body would permit—sprang to my feet and drew my pistol from the nightstand.

"I was wondering when you'd get home, Love..." said a distinctly feminine voice. To my surprise, the voice was not Kat's, but Lola's.

"What are you doing here?" I managed to say, only slightly slurring my words. I quickly switched on the light.

"I let myself in, while you were out. I couldn't stand to be all alone in my apartment—not with everything that's happened today. So I decided to stop by. When I saw you weren't home, I made myself comfortable."

She removed the covers. There she was, sprawled out over my bed, as naked as a newborn. Not a shred of modesty concealing her shapely body from my eyes. A voice in my head told me to kick her out, to tell her to get dressed, and get some sleep; but in my drunken state, another voice was making louder arguments in favor of the situation I found myself in.

"You shouldn't be here," I said, lowering my gun. "I told you; I'm seeing some—"

I lost my train of thought when she brushed her delicate fingers through her blonde locks and tucked a few strands behind her ear. At the same time, her smooth leg slid gracefully against the other, in a teasing and seductive manner.

"I've been thinking about us."

"There is no *us* anymore, Lola."

She ignored my statement.

"I know I made a mistake. I can't take it back, but I'm here now, trying to get things back to the way they were between us. I've missed you ... missed us."

She traced her finger along her stomach.

"I've seen how you look at me. You can deny it all you want, but deep down I know you miss this too. Don't you?"

My mind suddenly went blank. I found myself answering against my better judgment.

"Yes..."

She smiled coyly. Her blue eyes were locked with mine.

"The other night, you awakened something inside me while we were dancing. For a moment, it felt like nothing had changed. It made me think about all the things I missed while we were apart. We've missed so much.

"I want more of those moments with you. I made a stupid mistake—and it's not fair that I can't go back and change it, so we can be together again. When things ended between us, it felt as if a part of me was missing. After all this time, no one has come close to making me feel as whole as I do when I'm with you."

There were plenty of rational arguments floating around in the conscious part of my mind at that moment that would've put an end to this whole business before things went too far, but I was too tired and too drunk to listen to any of them. My thoughts were too focused on the naked dame in my bed to even care. I couldn't take my eyes off her.

Lola only smiled mischievously and allowed me to continue ogling her from where I was standing.

"Does this view bring back any pleasant memories," she mused. "It's all right. You can look. I don't mind."

She crawled over to the edge of the bed on her hands and knees; her hips swayed seductively as she did so. I could feel a heat rising inside me. It only grew as her naked form got closer to me.

"You know...we could *relive* a few of those memories right now...Maybe make a few new ones while we're at it."

Lola got off the bed and stepped forward, so she was standing in front of me—I had a clear view of everything. Her fingers slowly caressed my chest. I could smell the perfume on the nape of her neck as she moved closer still.

"You've been longing for this since I walked back through your door."

"Yes..." I answered.

"I've been waiting for this for so long. Don't worry, no one will find out about tonight. All I'm asking for is one more chance. I don't care if you're seeing someone else. Right now, it's just you and me. The rest of the world can wait. I know that you want this just as badly as I do. It'll be our little secret. No one else needs to know.

"Tonight, I want you all to myself. I don't care what happens next—Just give me this one last chance to show you how much I've missed you."

"Lola—"

Before I could object, her lips were on mine. To my surprise, I kissed her back. Any reservations, or thoughts of pulling away, vanished into our passionate kiss. I forgot all about Kat, and everyone else in the world. It was just the two of us.

Unbridling the deep forbidden desires I'd been keeping locked away for years, I swept Lola off her feet and tossed her back onto the bed, as we succumbed to our carnal pleasures.

After another session of love-making, Lola and I laid on the bed in silence; our bodies glistened with sweat. Lola had her hand across my chest and her left leg curled over both of mine. She was panting with a very satisfied look on her face:

"I forgot how good you were, Love..."

She placed the butt of a fresh cigarette between her lips.

"Do you have a light?"

I shook my head. "Must've left mine somewhere else earlier tonight."

I rolled over and reached into the nightstand drawer and retrieved a small box of matches from it.

"Here—use this," I said, striking the head of a match between my fingers and igniting the flame.

Lola leaned in toward it and poked the end of the cigarette into the flame until its end glowed red.

"Thanks, Love," she said, then blew a cloud of smoke in my direction, "You know, I wish we could do this more often. I thoroughly enjoyed that."

Once all the *hanky-panky* was over, I found myself thinking a bit more clearly.

"Don't get used to it, toots. This was a one-time thing," I assured her, "I'm—"

"Yeah, yeah...You're seeing that secretary in your office these days. I know," Lola said, rolling her eyes. "You don't need to say it again."

She puffed another cloud of smoke into the air and raised an eyebrow.

"Must be some special girl if you're still thinking of running back to her after the night we just had. I can see why you like her."

"Why's that?"

Lola smirked. "Because she's one halo short of being holy in this city of sinners. That girl's as wholesome as a nun at Sunday Mass. Unlike everyone else in this town, she's the only one not playing angles to get what she wants—Must be nice. She probably doesn't even realize that she's got everything already." There was a bitterness in her tone. "I'd kill to be in her shoes."

"If you say so..." I said with my back to her.

"Hmmm...I wonder...What do you think she would do if she saw us now? Do you think she'd react like you did when you caught me with Hill?" she pondered.

"That was different," I objected.

"Really? Hmm..."

As much as I hated to admit it, I was rowing in the same boat Lola had been in that night. Now, I was guilty of the same sin that I had demonized her for. I shifted uncomfortably, unwilling to admit my part in the recent betrayal.

"I mean what I said earlier: this was a *one-time thing*. After tonight, you and I are done. I want you out of here before I wake up.

"Don't bother swinging by the office tomorrow. I got my hands full there at the moment—and I don't want to see you. I'll drop you a line once I find your sister's killer, just like we arranged. You don't set foot in my office unless I say so from now on.

"Now, why don't you do us both a favor and make yourself scarce. I got a busy morning."

I heard Lola scoff as she exited the covers and gathered her belongings

"And Lola..." I added, "If I ever catch you breaking into my apartment again while I'm away, you'll be talking to the barrel of my gun and hear what it has to say about it."

Without another word, I closed my eyes, rolled over, and drifted off to sleep.

When I woke up that morning, I found myself alone in my apartment.

I clocked into the office a little after nine. Kat arrived a few minutes after I did. She threw her arms around me and kissed me, completely oblivious of the wrong I had done her earlier that night. I couldn't look her in the eyes without being struck by a wave of silent guilt and regret.

She quickly noticed the scars I'd gotten from my run-in with Ashes Burns.

"Oh my God—Look at the state you're in!" she said with visible concern. "What happened? Who did that to your handsome face?"

"No one," I told her, "just had a little run-in with a couple of trouble boys last night and got into an accident is all."

Her eyes widened.

"An accident?" she gasped, raising her voice. "What are you doing here? You should be at the hospital!"

"I'm fine."

"Those injuries say otherwise!" Kat carefully inspected the cuts on my face a little more closely. "Please tell me this wasn't from working the Desiree Case."

My silence gave her the answer she didn't want to hear.

"Guy, this case is getting to be too much for you. Maybe it's time to drop it and let someone else handle it. You're going to get yourself killed carrying on like this."

"I'll be fine," I said, my eyes did not meet her gaze.

Kat gestured to the telephone on my desk. "And what's going on with the man who keeps calling you? Is he someone who's involved in all this?"

I brushed her hands from my face and turned away from her. She was getting dangerously close to the truth. If she uncovered more than she needed to, she was going to find more of my dirty laundry than she bargained for.

"For your own good, Kat, stay out of this. I've got a handle on it."

Kat was sharp enough to put things together.

"So this *does* have something to do with Miss Desiree," she gathered.

"This has nothing to do with Lola—" The informal name slipped out before I could catch myself. It was too late; Kat had already heard it.

Her brow furrowed. "So it's *Lola* now. I thought you were going to keep things strictly business between you two."

"There's more at play here than you know about!" I explained.

"So then *tell* me!" she pleaded. "Help me understand!"

I let my shoulders drop. Deep down, I wanted to confess it all to her and come clean about what was really going on, but that wouldn't have done either of us any good.

"I-I can't..."

My response didn't satisfy her.

"Fine," she said, voicing her disappointment, "Keep your secrets. I don't understand why you still feel the need to keep them hidden from me. I'm not asking you to tell me all your secrets, but don't keep me in the dark about them either. All I ask is that you trust me with a few of the big ones every once in a while.

"I like to think that I've been an open book with you since I first walked through that door. I've only ever really kept one secret from you—but that's only because every time I've tried to tell you, something always comes up before I get the chance to."

"Tell me what?"

Kat shifted nervously.

"I-I'm pregnant..."

The news hit me like a ton of bricks. I turned around to make sure that I'd heard her correctly.

"Pregnant?" I repeated, mildly confused.

She nodded and gave a tiny nervous smile. "It's yours."

I was still trying to wrap my head around it all. Between everything that happened between Lola and I last night, trying to find Nerezza, and the new deadline Capone had given me to kill him; Kat's timing was not the best. Now I had to worry about a baby on top of everything; a baby that was growing inside the very same woman that Wyant had threatened to kill, not twenty-four hours earlier, if I botched the job for Capone again.

"Are you sure?"

There was absolute certainty in Kat's eyes when she nodded a second time.

"How long have you known?"

She shrugged. "About a month now. I didn't want to say anything until I knew where we stood in our relationship."

I quickly did the math in my head. Everything added up. It was definitely mine. This complicated things.

Kat seemed to sense that my thoughts were split on the matter.

"Guy? What's wrong? I thought you'd be happy."

Of course, I was happy, but now there was so much more at stake. Kat had just put me behind the eight ball without realizing it—A man could lose his marbles after being put under that kind of pressure. Still, I thought it was better to keep my dame's mind in a better state than my own.

"I am," I admitted. "It's just a lot to wrap my head around."

Kat stepped closer and took both my hands in hers.

"You're not mad at me, are you?" she asked innocently.

"No," I said, "of course not."

She threw her arms around me and gave me a firm squeeze. Her face was beaming with happiness; it was the most beautiful thing I'd seen.

"Good! I know you've been under a lot of stress lately. I just hoped that this would help ease some of your tension." — *It didn't*, but I wasn't about to tell her that.

She looked up at me with those bright blue eyes of hers.

"Guy..." Kat cooed.

"Yes?"

"I love you."

The memory of my recent betrayal made those words sting even more. I'd done her dirty and she didn't even know it. Hopefully, she never found out.

"I love you too," was all I could bring myself to say in response.

Kat rested her head against my chest.

"Everything will be all right..." she said as sweetly as an angel, "I promise."

The threat of Wyant's visit loomed in the back of my mind.

"I hope so, doll...I hope so..."

CHAPTER 13

Lost Things and Precious Moments

The clock was ticking.

Once Kat and I ended our tender embrace, I headed into my office to focus on devising a plan for how I was going to find and kill Alastor Nerezza. I decided to revisit the files I had on him and his known associates. I couldn't afford to waste my time focusing on the Desiree Case. Killing Nerezza had become a matter of life and death.

I stepped behind my desk to retrieve the files from the locked drawer. It was then that I noticed that the lock had been tampered with. The drawer slid open with the slightest touch; its once-secured contents had been removed.

"Kat..." I called.

She came at the sound of her name. "Yes, baby?"

"What time did you leave the office last night?"

Kat looked slightly perplexed.

"I closed up shortly after nine. Why?"

I continued to search around the office. "Because someone's broken into my desk and taken the files I had for the Desiree Case!"

The young woman was shocked. "What? I made sure that both doors were locked before I went home last night!"

I noticed the stack of papers that I'd set down by the fire escape window the night before had been knocked onto the floor. Upon closer inspection, I found evidence that someone had jimmied the window's lock too.

"They didn't come in through the door. They came in through the fire escape," I deduced. "They knew *exactly* where to find the files. They must've entered through the window, broke the lock, then climbed back down the fire escape with the files in hand as soon as they knew you were gone for the night."

Kat looked concerned. There was no way that she could've known that something like that was going to happen.

As she started to get down on her hands and knees, I stopped her. "It's no use, Kat. The files are gone."

The break-in only heightened my concern for Kat's safety.

"Do you still carry a pistol in your handbag?" I asked.

She nodded.

"Good. Make sure you keep it close to you at all times."

There was no use pretending there wasn't any danger. At least if she kept herself armed, she was not completely helpless. I wasn't taking any chances—not with all the hubbub going around. Things were getting dangerous with each passing moment.

The first order of business was to fix the window latch before we had any more unwelcome visitors. I pointed over to the closet.

"Kat, do me a favor...Open the closet there and look for a leather workbag on the floor."

Kat did as she was told. A moment later, she held up the brown leather workbag I was looking for.

"Good girl. Now bring it over here and set it on my desk."

Once the bag was on my desk, I opened it; revealing the assortment of tools inside. I grabbed a screwdriver and began replacing the broken latch on the window.

"Until I fix this window, we're not seeing any clients today. Understand?"

Kat agreed and walked into the other room, while I made the repairs.

Fixing the window was duck soup. I had the old latch removed and the new one installed in just under an hour—the drawer lock was a different story. It would have to be replaced completely; lucky for me, there was nothing important in that drawer left to lock up.

I placed the bag of tools back in the closet when I finished up, then leaned against the door frame and watched Kat. She was busy at her desk typing up documents and filing them in the cabinet behind her, but that was not what I saw.

The only thing that caught my attention was how beautiful she looked. Something about the way she moved, made her seem like she was glowing brightly. Pregnancy agreed with her.

She could've been wearing a dress made out of a paper bag and I still would've called her the most beautiful woman in the world. It would've been true. Kat had the looks of an angel and the heart to match; innocent and pure.

At that moment, I knew when all this was over, I'd settle down with her and take her as far away from Chicago as I could. We'd find a house somewhere quiet, where we could raise our little family away from Capone and every other gangster in the world. My mind was made up on the matter.

That was all I ever wanted: a fresh start. Kat was the answer to that.

I couldn't tell if Kat knew I was watching her—If she did, she pretended not to notice. Every so often, I'd catch a quick glimpse of a smile at the corner of her mouth while she worked. If I could've stopped time, I would've made that moment last forever.

Thankfully, she didn't have the slightest inkling of what happened between Lola and I prior to that morning. I didn't even want to think about the trouble that knowledge would've dug up if she ever found out about my infidelity, it would've broken her heart.

The clock continued ticking like the echoing footsteps of a condemned man on his way to the hangman's noose. With the very real possibility of death looming over our heads, I began to realize that any plans I was pushing off for the future would be too late. There were things I couldn't leave unsaid.

"Kat..."

She gave me her full attention. "Yes?"

"There's something that I've been wanting to talk to you about. I was going to tell you after I finished up the Desiree Case, but I don't think a thing like this can wait..."

I started searching my head for the right words to use.

"I was wondering...What do you think about the two of us getting hitched?"

Kat's jaw dropped with enough space to park a car in it.

"Are you—Did you—" she started, still trying to process the question, "Are you asking me to marry you?"

I shrugged. "Well, what do you say, doll?"

A huge smile broke across her lips. It was soon followed by a steady stream of tears. She practically hurtled over the desk and into my arms.

"Yes!" she cried, "Yes! Yes! And a million times, yes!"

I held Kat in my arms and tilted her back for a deep kiss. When it broke, both of us had to take a moment to catch our breath.

"Oh, Guy! You don't know how happy I am to hear that!"

It was my turn to smile. Her beaming smile was infectious.

"Now, I don't have a ring or anything," I confessed, "but I was thinking, what'd you say we close up for a few hours so you and I can go pick one out right now?"

Kat had her coat on before I even finished asking my question. The two of us were out the door shortly after.

As I helped Kat into the passenger seat of my car, I noticed a figure lurking behind us at the far corner of the sidewalk; I immediately recognized the man as Marcus Wyant.

I climbed into the driver's seat and drove away—the entire time keeping my eyes fixed on Wyant's reflection in the rearview mirror.

CHAPTER 14

Chance Meetings

I lost track of the number of rings that Kat tried on. She marveled at each of them as they hung on her delicate finger. To her, she was in a world of sparkling stars—All I saw was a bunch of overpriced rocks attached to a small metal band. We must have been in there for an hour, at the very least.

Finally, Kat picked out a small round finger decoration with a stone the size of a pea. It was modest but still managed to catch the eye in the right light—not unlike Kat. She was not one for overly flashy things, instead choosing to enjoy the simplistic beauty of things that most people overlooked. If it had been Lola I was shopping for, the ice on the end of the band would've had to have been no smaller than a strawberry—thankfully, Kat was not so vain.

I looked at the ring she had picked out. It looked like it had been made for her finger. It was neither too tight, nor too loose; *a perfect fit*. The white gold band complemented her fairer skin tone nicely without drawing too much attention to it. Better still was the fact that it was fairly inexpensive in comparison to the others she had looked at.

I picked out a ring for myself that was similar to hers—one that didn't cost me an arm or a leg either. I wasn't too concerned with what it looked like, the only thing that mattered was that it showed just how committed I was to Kat.

After placing it on the fourth finger of my left hand, I paid the jeweler for our pair of rings. The entire trip from the counter to the door, Kat kept going on about how "perfect" and "beautiful" her ring was. Eventually, I realized she wasn't really talking to me; more so herself, than to anyone in particular.

Just as we exited the shop, I heard a familiar voice:

"Duncan—Funny bumping into you here. What are the chances?" called Marcus Wyant.

Kat and I turned to see the large man walking toward us like an old pal.

He was dressed in a dark grey suit with a slightly darker overcoat and a matching Homburg hat atop his enormous melon. The sickening grin on Wyant's face indicated that his appearance was far from just a chance encounter. He walked like a man who owned the block; boorish and arrogant.

I narrowed my eyes at his approach. "What are you doing here, Wyant?" I asked.

Capone's muscle shrugged. "I just happened to be in the area running some errands—you know how it is—when I spotted you from across the street there. Figured I'd swing over and say hello."

He looked over at Kat and adjusted the gutter crown on his head:

"Who might this ripe little tomato be?" His smile took on a more menacing appearance.

I pushed my way between Wyant and Kat.

"None of your business."

"Is that how you're going to treat an old pal in front of your dame?" he said, shaking his head in disappointment, "I'm hurt. And here I thought you'd be civil enough to introduce us?"

"Keep talking, and the only thing I'll introduce is a hard knuckle to the side of your face," I warned.

"Guy Duncan!" Kat scolded, "There's no need to be rude!" She turned back to Wyant. "I'm sorry. I'm his fiancée, Kathrine Stevens. You must be Mr. Wyant. I recognized your voice from your calls to the office."

Wyant raised both his hairy eyebrows in delight.

"His fiancée..." he repeated, shooting me a look that spelled trouble. "Well then, I guess congratulations are in order. You be sure to keep this one safe, Duncan. Would be a shame if something happened to her."

I wanted to sock Wyant in the jaw and wipe that smug grin off his face—but Kat was there, so I didn't. If I'd done anything then, there was a good chance she would've gotten hurt. Reluctantly, I pressed those feelings deep down and kept a cool head.

I scowled at him. "I'll do that."

Kat and I turned around and began to walk away; I put an arm around her to keep her close.

We were ten steps away before Wyant called after us again:

"Oh and Duncan..."

I stopped and glared at him over my shoulder.

"Don't go forgetting about that job we talked about." He gestured to his wristwatch. "The clock's still ticking."

Having nothing more to say to Wyant, I turned and continued walking away with my arm around Kat. She looked at me with a confused look on her face:

"What job?"

I tried to shrug the question off.

"It's nothing. Let's go get you a new dress for the big day," I said, changing the subject.

Kat spent a whole hour looking at all the white dresses in the dress shop. She was like a girl with a bad sweet tooth in a candy shop. There were dresses made of lacey silk, rayon, and even some made of satin. Kat excitedly tried on several of them—though, she refused to let me see her in any of the dresses until the wedding.

While she was trying on a series of expensive-looking dresses, I made my way over to the front window and cautiously kept an eye out to make sure Wyant wasn't still tailing us. It was bad enough that we'd run into him earlier—I didn't feel like running into him a second time.

His threat was at the forefront of my mind. Unlike most of the apes in this city that went around puffing their chest and making idle threats, Wyant actually had the means to cash them in.

I impatiently looked down at the ticking timepiece on my wrist; it was nearly noon. If I was going to keep Kat from getting hurt, I needed to get moving. I'd considered peeking into the changing room to get things moving faster, but I knew that would only merit a firm scolding from the dame on the other side of the door if I had.

You can imagine how relieved I was when Kat exited the changing room with a white box tucked under her arm. The box had a gold ribbon tied around it neatly—no doubt containing the dress she'd chosen inside it.

"You decide on one?" I asked.

"I sure did," she giggled. "Can't wait for you to see me in it."

I smiled. "I'm sure you'll be a dish in that dress. I won't be able to keep my eyes off you."

She giggled again. "You can barely keep your eyes off me now as it is."

We approached the cashier—a woman around Kat's age, with raven-black hair—and set the box on the counter. She then asked if we'd found everything we were looking for—I sincerely hoped so and found myself very relieved when Kat said she had.

Then came the moment I was least looking forward to; paying for a dress I hadn't even seen yet. It was much more expensive than I'd anticipated—a hefty $59.53. I bit the bullet and handed the money over to the cashier. Even though the steep price hurt the wallet, it was an expense I was willing to pay to make Kat happy.

After leaving the dress shop, Kat and I made our way back over to the car. As bad as running into Wyant was, it was duck soup compared to who spotted us next.

"Guy?" asked Lola Desiree, picking me out in the bustling crowd of people walking about. When she was certain it was me, she approached us. "I thought it was you, Love."

She noticed Kat and looked visibly disappointed—and even disgusted—to see her standing beside me.

"Oh—You're here too." The words seemed sour on her tongue and appropriately matched the expression on her face.

Both women eyed each other like two felines fighting over the same ball of yarn. I could feel the tension between them growing. Neither spoke for a moment, but Lola was the first to break the silence:

"What brings you out here ... with your *squeeze*?" The question was directed at me. "I thought you'd be busy at the office."

Before I could answer, Kat cut in:

"Oh, we were...but then, Guy asked me to marry him this morning," she said, proudly displaying the ring on her finger to the rival dame. "We just finished buying my wedding dress."

"Is that so..." Lola said with jealous interest, "Well, aren't you the lucky girl."

I was half expecting Lola to spill the beans on our nocturnal session of *hanky-panky* to Kat then and there; to my surprise, she did not. Instead, she gave a warm smile.

"Congratulations," she said. "These days, it's hard to come by a loyal man like Guy here. Most of the men I know in this city have an extra *squeeze* they're seeing on the side."

Lola's eyes trailed over to mine as if to remind me of my latest sins.

"Any leads on my sister's killer?" she added, changing the focus of the conversation.

I welcomed the new topic. "Not at present. Like I told you yesterday, I'll drop you a line if there are any more developments."

Not wanting to take any more chances with Lola, I opened the passenger door for Kat. "Now, if you'll excuse us. We need to be on our way."

The blonde dame pouted. "Oh, so soon? All right. I guess I'll see you soon. Ta-ta!"

Lola gave a quick wave as I started the engine and pulled away.

CHAPTER 15

A Little Slice of Heaven

Kat and I returned to the office around two-fifteen, or so. After performing a quick sweep of both rooms, I determined everything was just as we had left it. Once I was satisfied with the search, I hung our coats on the rack beside Kat's desk and looked over at her.

She looked like she was over the moon about the whole situation. I'm sure she was still coming to terms with all the excitement. I'll admit, I was still coming to terms with it myself. Needless to say, Kat was in heaven.

"Is this day real or am I still dreaming?" she sighed.

"It's real," I assured her.

Her smile brightened.

"Have I told you how much I love you?"

I returned the smile and pulled her closer. "You have, but why don't you remind me again, doll." I planted a big one on her lips.

In a city of backstabbing devils and shady sinners, I can't tell you how rare it is for a guy in my line of work to find himself a little slice of heaven that he can call his own. For the first time in my life, I'd found the one person who shed some light in a world of darkness. Come to think of it, I don't think I've ever been that happy before Kat walked through my door.

We broke the kiss; Kat needed a moment to catch her breath. Her chest rose and fell with each breath she took. Her heart was beating as fast as a drummer playing the skins. She lifted her hand and gently ran her fingers through my hair.

"What's going through that head of yours, handsome?"

I peered into those gentle blue eyes and smiled.

"I was just thinking...Why do we have to wait? What would you say if I told you I wanted to marry you tomorrow?"

I'd piqued her interest. She raised a brow. "I'd say, why wait until tomorrow when we can just head down to the courthouse tonight."

As much as I wanted to jump at the opportunity, all this would be for nothing if I didn't finish my job for Capone first.

"My night's a little booked tonight," I admitted, "I'm needed elsewhere. But tonight, why don't you put on that dress tonight and wait for me to get back tomorrow morning? That way, you and I can just head down to the courthouse without wasting any time getting ready."

The notion made Kat as excited as a schoolgirl. She clapped her hands together gleefully.

"Oh, Guy, that would be perfect!"

She threw her arms around me with such force that I nearly tumbled backward.

"All right then. It's settled. I'll swing by the office and pick you up tomorrow morning."

"I'll be *Mrs. Guy Duncan* before breakfast," she reveled.

"Come rain or shine," I added.

It turned out fate decided it would be the former. Just then, I heard the light tapping of droplets dance on the window; slow at first, then faster, until it became a downpour. Thunder rumbled in the distance. Judging by the way it was coming down, it didn't seem like it was going away anytime soon.

Time was ticking. I needed to focus on how I was going to get close enough to Nerezza to finish the job. It was still too early to head down to the docks, but that gave me plenty of time to prepare. My slice of heaven with Kat would have to wait a little longer.

"You'll have to excuse me, kitten. There are a few things I need to look into before I head out tonight." I glanced out the window again at the storm outside. "Looks like it's going to be a miserable night. It's cats and dogs out there."

Kat looked out the window, only then, noticing the change in the weather.

"You're right. It's really coming down." She looked at me with the eyes of a begging kitten. "Are you sure you have to head out into it tonight?"

I nodded.

"I'm sure. Unfortunately, I have a deadline I can't afford to miss tonight. Besides, a little rain never bothered me."

She frowned, but deep down I knew she understood.

I gently kissed her forehead, before heading into my office. It was time to get back to work.

For the next couple of hours, I drew an outline of the factory's layout on a piece of paper on my desk. It wasn't hard to include the parts of it that I had already seen. With a little guesswork, I was able to fill in the sections the sketch was missing.

After what had gone down the night before, I was certain that Nerezza had doubled his security that night. It was going to be much harder to sneak into the guarded factory a second time. I'd have to wait until I got there before I could find a way in.

I placed a few extra clips in the pockets of my suit jacket and holstered the loaded Savage in my hand. I wanted to make sure I was prepared if I found myself deep in dutch.

I glanced over at the clock on the wall; it was half-past-nine. The hours had flown by. It was time to get the job over with, so I could finally put an end to my business with Capone for good.

The only thing that worried me was dealing with Nerezza's goons when I got there. Killing Nerezza was one thing—hell, I probably could've taken on Agresta myself if I really had to—but going up against a small army of his goons on my own was something else entirely.

I needed a backup plan if things went south. An idea popped into my head a moment later.

I stepped over to the telephone on my desk and made one more call, grabbed my hat and coat, then headed out the door.

CHAPTER 16

Wet Feet and the Brewing Storm

It was dark when I pulled up to the factory around ten-thirty. I parked the car in an empty boat shed three blocks from the building and continued the rest of the way on foot.

As I expected, Nerezza had doubled his security for the night. The untimely death of Ashes Burns had made him realize that he wasn't as safe as he thought he was. There were booze guards at every one of the building's entrances, all armed with a lot more kick than the Savage I was packing.

I crept over to the west side of the factory, where I found rows of wooden crates stacked up high that created several aisles near the docks. Everything was soaked to the brim, as the heavy rain continued; the towers of crates did little to shelter me from it. I quickly ducked behind a small pile of unstacked crates as I heard voices approaching.

There were two guards patrolling there, making sure no strays wandered onto the premises. They paused a few rows from where I was hiding. I held my breath and pressed my drenched body against the shadows the crates created to avoid being seen.

The first guard turned to his companion:

"I'm cold," he grumbled through chattering teeth. "I don't get why we have to be outside in this mess."

"Quit your bellyaching and keep your eyes open," the other guard said gruffly.

"You sure all this security isn't a bit much?"

"Don't be a bunny, Jimmy. After last night's break-in, the boss wants to make sure no one else stumbles into this place and messes with the shipments. Burns didn't even get the ones from last night out because of it."

"I heard Old Ashes Burns croaked while chasing whoever paid us a visit. They said his body was so burnt that the coppers had trouble identifying him when they first found him a few miles from here."

The second guard shrugged. "I wouldn't know. I wasn't working last night. Still, that's a rough way to go. But let me tell you, the boss was not happy when he found out his shipments didn't get delivered. I imagine a few heads are going to roll because of it."

"Is it true that the boss has been in his office all day?" asked the first.

The companion turned to the other man with a look of annoyance on his face.

"Do you *really* think we'd be out here freezing our keisters off while it's pouring cats and dogs if the boss wasn't here? No. We would not!"

That confirmed my suspicions; Nerezza was inside. As soon as I found a way into the factory, I'd know exactly where to look for him. I wasn't going to get anywhere, though, with those two goons standing guard. I needed a distraction.

I felt around on the ground for something I could use that wouldn't raise the alarm; using my pistol would've brought the whole factory down on me. Just then, my hand brushed against the hook of a crowbar near one of the crates behind me. *Perfect!*

I quietly tucked the end of the tool under the thin gap of one of the crates and pried the lid open. Inside, was a dozen bottles of bathtub gin. I decided that would have to do.

After carefully lifting one of the bottles from its casing, I popped the cork open and took a generous swig of the hooch. It wasn't bad—it wasn't great either—but it was sure to put some hair on my chest.

I wiped my mouth with my sleeve before I recorked the bottle and tossed it away from the guards. The loud *crash* of glass startled both of them. They immediately lifted their gats.

"What was that?"

"It came from over there." The other man pointed in the direction I'd thrown the bottle. "Go check it out."

The first guard headed toward where the sound had come from. He held his gun in one hand and a bright torch in the other. He looked both nervous and prepared to squirt metal at whatever he found. The light in his hand danced from side to side while he searched the aisle nearest me.

As he got closer to my hiding spot, I grabbed a pebble off the ground and tossed it further down the aisle behind me, drawing the man's attention in a new direction.

The guard pointed the torch into the aisle and cautiously continued forward; walking past the stack of crates where I was hiding.

I slowly crept out from behind the crates; taking care to keep my footsteps as quiet as possible, while dodging any puddles that I encountered along the way; and tiptoed my way behind the guard.

Once I was close enough, I slugged him in the back of the head with the crowbar.

The man collapsed onto the wet ground with a loud *thud!* He was sleeping like a newborn a moment later—a very *ugly* newborn.

I tucked my arms under the man's shoulders and dragged his limp body behind another stack of crates so it was out of view.

A few minutes passed by silently. The only noise that was heard was the rain as it continued to fall. When the first man failed to return, his companion decided to investigate.

"Jimmy? You find anything?"

No reply.

"Come on, Jimmy. You know how my heart is these days. You better not be hiding somewhere, waiting to jump out at me, like you did a few weeks ago. That's a good way to get a cap right between the eyes."

There was still no reply.

The remaining guard continued into the same aisle where "Jimmy" had disappeared. He spotted the bright hand torch on the ground; its bulb still shining across the wet pavement.

Before he had the chance to turn around, I jumped out from my hiding place and whacked him across the side of his head with the butt-end of his friend's gun. His body dropped to the ground like a bag of bricks.

After I had moved both bodies out of view, I was clear to head toward the west side entrance of the factory. To my disappointment, that entrance was still being guarded by two other thugs who were much burlier than the last pair I encountered. I wasn't going to be able to get in that way, so I looked around for another way in.

Rounding the corner near that same door, I spotted a window that was open slightly. As I observed it more closely, I noticed one of the hinges was so rusted that it was a miracle it was still attached at all. By the looks of it, it was in such bad shape that the window didn't close completely. *That was my ticket in.*

I carefully slid the base of the window open a little; it only opened about halfway. Luckily, that was just enough space to slide through it—though, it was still a tight squeeze.

Once I was completely inside, I lowered the window again. I looked down at my feet; there was a large puddle of water accumulating on the ground. I cursed silently to myself and looked around; there was nothing lying about that I could use to clean it up. I just hoped no one noticed the puddle near the window.

I continued down a narrow hallway until I found myself in what I could only assume was the factory's garage. Inside, I noticed about five, or so, delivery trucks being loaded up with crates similar to the ones I'd seen outside.

Before I could continue on, one of the goons loading the truck noticed me:

"Hey, you, where'd you come from?"

I held my breath and gripped the rifle in my hand more tightly—I kept my finger on the trigger as an added precaution.

"Hey, buddy, I'm talking to you. Are you deaf, or something? Where'd you come from?" the man asked again.

"Just got done walking the perimeter outside. I was passing through to find the dummy who was supposed to take over for me when I finished up," I lied.

The thug looked me up and down. He seemed convinced. "I don't envy any poor bastard who has to be out there tonight."

"Yeah," I said, "that makes two of us."

I turned to leave, but was stopped by the man once again:

"While you're here, mind giving us a hand loading this crate?"

I shook my head. "I don't know. I should really get—"

"It'll only take a minute."

Reluctantly, I agreed.

I quickly set the rifle down before I walked over and helped four other thugs lift a heavy crate into the back of one of the trucks—I could only assume it contained a shipment of guns in it, based on its weight and size. Once the crate was loaded, I slipped away down the adjacent hallway before they could enlist my help again.

After proceeding down the hallway, I found myself in the same room Sid and I were in the night before, where we'd first seen Agresta and Burns together. By the looks of it, Nerezza's bootleg shipments had never made it out that night—all the wooden crates we'd seen then, were still in the same places they'd been stacked before, with many more crates piled around them.

There was no shortage of workers on the shopfloor. Many of them performed the strenuous duties necessary for brewing the illegal hooch; some supervised the steel tanks and vats in the center of the room, while others bottled and packed the gin into additional crates for shipping.

THE DEVIL YOU KNOW

Realizing I'd left myself unarmed after my hasty departure from the garage, I cautiously drew my pistol from the inside of my pocket—there was no immediate threat, but you and I both know how quickly that can change.

Before anyone saw me, I ducked behind one of the larger stacks of crates and scanned the upper level for Nerezza's office. Above my head, there were eight heavily armed booze guards walking along the catwalks, making sure none of the workers slacked off.

My eyes were suddenly drawn to a lone door on the second level. The thick wooden door was guarded by four heavyset thugs; two of them were packing Thompsons. That was all the evidence I needed.

I looked around for a way up.

Within spitting distance was a staircase connected to one of the catwalks. The problem was, doing so, meant crossing the shopfloor with no cover before I reached it.

It was risky. Even if I managed to reach it and somehow get up to the second level, I'd be made the moment I reached the top. The other routes did not look any better. In every scenario, I considered, there were none where I reached the catwalk without getting a bad case of lead poisoning. I cursed myself for forgetting the guard's rifle in the garage; it would've saved me some trouble then.

Unfortunately, it was too late to double back and retrieve it. I decided that I'd have to take my chances armed only with the pistol in my hand.

Before I had the chance to try anything, I felt a hard impact against the back of my skull. After that, the world went black.

CHAPTER 17

The Devil's Hour

I awoke with a throbbing headache and a lump the size of a golf ball on the back of my head. Whoever had gotten the jump on me had fists like steel. I moved to rub the lump, only to find my hands had been tied behind my back with some rope.

Shapes around the dark room began to come into focus a bit more clearly than they had before. On the far side of the room was a lit fireplace. There was no rug on the ground like the office at the Drake, instead, all of the floorboards were on clear display—some more crooked than others. Four shelves of books lined the wall behind a desk made of rich serpentine mahogany.

As I became more aware of my surroundings, I realized two things: I was tied to a chair in an office, and I wasn't there alone. When the room finally stopped spinning, I found myself face-to-face with Otis Agresta.

The tall intimidating man smiled at me, with all but good intentions.

"You've been out cold for three hours. I was beginning to think Otis had killed you when he caught you snooping around my factory," said a voice that definitely didn't belong to Agresta: It was Alastor Nerezza.

The rising crime boss sat casually behind his desk. The lit cigar in his mouth glowed a bright red at the tip and a cloud of smoke exited his lips slowly.

I glanced over at the clock on the wall: it was one-forty-five in the morning. I'd been out for a little more than three hours.

"Comfortable?" Nerezza asked. "Well, now that you're awake, can I offer you a drink?"

His sadistic grin made my skin crawl. After what happened the last time I accepted a drink from him, I would never make that same mistake again. I shook my head.

"I had one on the way over. I should stay sober enough to drive myself home later," I said, turning down the invitation.

Agresta chuckled. "What makes you think we're going to let you make it home at all."

Nerezza remained behind his desk and took another puff of his cigar. It was dark and hard to see him in the dim light. He switched on a desk lamp, which made it easier to see him. Unlike the last time I saw him, Nerezza was not dressed to impress the public; he was dressed for shady business.

He was wearing a grey tailored suit, the color of dirty snow, with a tie as black as night around his neck. His hair was slicked back in its usual fashion. The gangster removed the cigar from his mouth and set it on an ashtray on his desk. He was reading something, but I couldn't see what it was until he held it up.

"Quite the file you've put together here, Mr. Duncan. I must say, I'm impressed." Nerezza revealed the missing files from my office in his hand. "You've done your homework on us—Hmm...There's even a file on you, Otis. Lots of dangerous information in here that could be trouble if it fell into the wrong hands."

I scowled at him. "So it was *you* who broke into my office last night!"

The mob boss stood up with both files still in his hand.

"Oh, I can assure you, I did not set foot in your office. My informant was kind enough to deliver these files to me this morning." He walked around his desk and flipped through the files again. "Don't look so surprised. I have more than a few sources at my disposal that allowed me to retrieve these files. It looks like my informant brought me everything you had on me."

Nerezza walked over to the fireplace and dropped the stolen files into the flames. The paper folders were ash in less than a minute.

"You can't be too careful these days," he said, as he returned to his desk.

I watched as all the dirt I gathered on the two criminals standing before me literally went up in smoke. Nerezza continued:

"I'm not interested in who gave you your information. What does interest me, however, is the fact that you ignored the warning I gave you the other night.

"I let you walk away with your life, and this is how you repay my generosity? I'm hurt."

He rubbed his ringed fingers to his furrowed brow.

"I was willing to overlook your interest in me—but then, you had to go and kill one of my most trusted associates. Because of you, my shipments never made it out last night. It's bad for business.

"I don't take too kindly to those who make it a habit of gumming up my business. That kind of insolence cannot go unpunished."

He nodded to Agresta, who immediately delivered two powerful punches into my stomach.

I felt the air rush out of my lungs from the impact. A heavy cough escaped my mouth. It was like getting hit with the same brick twice. Once the coughing subsided, it took me a moment to catch my breath.

Nerezza motioned for Agresta to hold his assault on my body for the moment. He slowly walked toward me, while still maintaining a safe distance.

"I wasn't born yesterday. I know a *dropper* when I see one. Someone sent you here to whack me, didn't they?"

He found his answer in my defiant silence.

"Of course they did," he continued, "I got plenty of competition in this city that'd love to see me sleeping with the fishes. So here's what's going to happen: I'm going to ask you a question and you're going to tell me who sent you. Then, I'm going to kill you. You get me?"

Nerezza bent forward a little closer so that he was almost eye-level with me:

"Who're you working for? Capone? Moran? Johnny Torrio? The coppers down at City Hall? Who sent you?"

I kept my trap shut. I noticed a muscle in Nerezza's forehead twitch. He was not happy with my answer—or lack of one.

He looked away and nodded to Agresta again.

The tower of muscle punched me repeatedly like he was tenderizing a slab of meat. A short time later, he was given the signal to stop again.

"I'm going to ask you again, son; *Who hired you?*" he demanded.

Once again, I didn't break. I was giving him nothing and it was driving him bananas.

The mob boss angrily ran his hands over his hair, slicking it back tighter. He turned to Agresta; his patience spent:

"See if you can loosen his lips. I don't care how you get him to talk, but I want him alive." He turned his attention back to me. "Maybe an hour with Otis will jog your memory."

With that, he exited his office, leaving the two of us alone.

Agresta smiled wickedly at me as he removed his tweed jacket and tossed it aside. He looked like a man poised on getting revenge. He cracked his knuckles and stretched his arms; I spied my Savage tucked into his trousers, near the leather belt around his waist.

The confidence and pride he took in dishing out pain, was as clear as the crooked nose on his face.

"Look at you, Otis," I said unimpressed. "Attacking an unarmed man tied to a chair. You must feel *real* tough."

Agresta said nothing in response, so I continued to prod until I struck a nerve.

"What would Lexi say if she could see you now?"

The mention of his late dame's name was enough to get his attention.

"You don't get to mention her name, pal. She's dead. This is nothing compared to what I'm going to do to whoever killed her. It'll be a closed casket funeral when I'm done with them."

He changed the topic:

"I'm guessing you were the one who bumped off Ashes last night. That was a big mistake. I'm going to enjoy every second of the beating I'm going to give you. Just you wait."

Agresta continued to use me as a punching bag. He started with a powerful right hook to my jaw, which he followed with an equally powerful left hook soon after. I felt the taste of blood fill my mouth. I spat it onto the floor.

"That all you got?" I said, egging him on.

The tall man threw another punch right into my ribcage. I gasped for breath as he hit me again.

"Who hired you to kill Mr. Nerezza?" he asked between punches.

I only smiled, letting some blood run onto the floor from my bottom lip.

He struck me across the face.

"Who're you working for?"

When I didn't answer, he hit me again.

Agresta poured more and more malice into each punch he threw my way. Every cell in my body roared with pain as the beating continued.

It was getting so intense that I was starting to fade in and out of consciousness.

Eventually, I stopped hearing the questions altogether. The only thing going through my head was Kat.

I could picture her smiling face gazing at me with the warmth of her loving blue eyes. I imagined the feeling of her gently raking her fingers through my hair and felt the sensation wash over my scalp. I heard the melodic tone of her tender voice, as it caressed my ears with sweet nothings.

While my body was being put through hell, whatever fraction of a soul I had left, was in complete bliss. I had no clue where I was at that moment. All I knew, was that Kat had followed me to whatever plane of existence my mind had wandered off to...and I didn't want to be anywhere else.

For the next hour, Agresta gave me the Broderick. His fists were covered in my blood.

My nose and lip were a fountain of red. My left eye was swollen shut and I was bruised in more places than I could count. It even hurt to breathe—I was sure that at least three of my ribs were either cracked or broken—and my muscles felt like they were on fire.

Despite all that, I gave him nothing.

I slowly regained consciousness when the beating had come to a halt. Out of my good eye, I saw the blurry shapes of Nerezza and Agresta come back into focus. I peeked over at the clock on the wall: it was two-forty-five.

Nerezza frowned at the sight of me.

"Christ, Otis! I said, I wanted him *alive*! Look at him!"

"He's still ticking," the thug assured him, "His jaw may be a bit busted up, but he's still breathing."

"Did you get him to sing for you?"

Agresta shook his head. "Not a tune. I've never seen a man take a beating like that and not crack. He's a tough nut this one."

While the two of them were talking, I wiggled my wrist—which hurt like hell—-and felt the small pocketknife I kept in my sleeve, drop into the palm of my hand. I carefully used my other hand to open the blade and started sawing at the rope. Neither of the gangsters got wise to what I was doing.

Nerezza stepped closer to me:

"Looks like you're a hard man to crack, Mr. Duncan. I'm starting to think we should just kill you."

I shifted forward uncomfortably on the seat of the chair.

"Like...you killed... his dame?" I wheezed to the crime boss, out of the least swollen side of my mouth.

Nerezza put a hand to his ear. "What was that? I didn't catch that. You should speak up."

I let out a cough and spat some of the blood in my mouth onto the floor in front of me.

"I said: just like you killed Lexi Desiree," I repeated, more clearly.

Agresta looked over at his boss. There was a large degree of confusion on his face.

"What's he talking about?"

Nerezza deflected the question. "Nothing. You must've knocked his melon one too many times. He's talking nonsense."

The tall goon's eyes looked over at me once before he turned to face Nerezza directly. The small cogs were turning in his mouse-sized brain.

"You...You killed my Lexi?" he said, putting the pieces together.

"Of course not!" his boss denied angrily. "Are you going looney?"

There appeared to be a new crack in Agresta's loyalty. I decided to use that shaken trust to my advantage.

"No...He just ordered one of his button men to blow her down for him behind your back."

A clear picture was beginning to form in Agresta's head. He tightened his fists and took a step toward his boss.

Nerezza, on the other hand, attempted to reason with the brute.

"Otis...you're not thinking clearly..." he said, taking a step back. "Let's just take a second and calm down. We'll talk about this once we've dealt with Duncan."

Agresta wasn't listening. His mind was only focused on his vendetta against his dame's killer. He took one step forward for every step his boss—or rather; former boss—took backward.

"Who was it?" Otis asked, with hellfire behind his eyes, "Who'd you send to ice my Lexi?"

"What does it matter? She was just some dame that was making you soft." Nerezza was treading deep water with the towering thug. "She was a nobody."

"She was my dame!" Otis roared. "And you killed her!"

He drew my Savage from his belt and pointed the business end of it at Nerezza.

"Who was it?" he demanded.

I quickened my pace and sawed faster, while their focus was on each other. There were only a few threads left in the rope around my hands.

"Otis..." Nerezza said, taking one more step back until he was standing beside his desk. "I promise...It was nothing personal..."

He quickly grabbed the pistol on his desk and fired it before Agresta could pull the trigger.

BANG!

The bullet in his chamber exited the barrel with a flash and struck Otis square in the forehead.

The thug's body suddenly toppled backward onto the floor; my pistol slid across the floorboards and landed at my feet.

"...It's just business."

At that very moment, I finished cutting the last threads of the rope, picked my pistol off the floor, and immediately pointed it at Nerezza.

The crime boss smiled and turned his pistol so that it was pointed at me.

"You've caused me a lot of trouble, Duncan. Now, you're going to pay for it."

The sound of gunfire suddenly erupted from outside the factory. Raised voices of goons scrambled in panic, as they returned fire.

The disturbance caught Nerezza completely off-guard.

"What's that? What have you done?" he shouted.

I cocked a smile out of the better side of my mouth.

"That would be Detective Hill and his backup. I told them *exactly* where to find your little operation here. If they didn't hear from me by three, they had orders to swarm the place."

Nerezza scowled at me. The look in his eye told me he wanted nothing more than to end my life.

The distant sound of gunfire was not so distant anymore. It echoed through the halls and continued getting closer and closer.

The crime boss nervously looked from me to the door several times; as if he were debating whether to use the next couple of seconds he had left to shoot me or make a run for it. He chose the latter.

Nerezza made a mad dash for the door.

I fired at him twice; the first shot missed and hit the wall behind him, while the second, passed through the meat of his arm as he hurried through the door. I quickly followed him a second later.

The guards that had been standing outside Nerezza's office, had been called elsewhere to deal with the new disturbance, leaving Nerezza alone on the catwalk.

I was on his tail.

As he booked it across the catwalk, I unloaded eight more slugs into his back, until my chamber was empty.

Nerezza staggered in place for a moment, then used his free hand to try and steady himself against the railing. But in the end, his body slipped over the metal bar and tumbled into the boiling vat of alcohol that awaited him below.

I limped over to where the late crime boss had fallen and peered over the railing.

The stiff was floating face down in the very liquid he dealt in. A sea of ruby poured out of it and contaminated the contents of the bubbling liquor. No one would be making a profit off the next batch of gin from that place for a while.

A labored sigh escaped my lips. It was done. Alastor Nerezza was dead. My debt with Capone was squared.

"Duncan? Duncan!" I heard Hill call, as he and a squad of armed officers, spilled into the shopfloor.

He hurried up the staircase and joined me on the catwalk.

"Where's Nerezza?"

I gestured to the vat below with my chin. "He rabbited, so I had to put him down."

The dick looked down and shook his head. He nearly gagged as the scent of the boiling corpse hit his nostrils.

"I was hoping to bring him in still breathing," he said, trying his best to ignore the growing stench. "We wanted to find out who he was doing business with, so we could nail them too."

The smell became too much to ignore.

"Christ—That stinks!" he coughed, fanning his nose.

I pointed over to the door to Nerezza's office. "I'm sure your boys will find his books in his office. Those should give you all the information you're after."

Hill nodded. "Good call. I'll have the boys stash those with the rest of the evidence before we leave."

He looked over at me.

"I was a little surprised when you called me about this place earlier. I thought you didn't like cops—me, least of all. Why the sudden change of heart?"

"You were the lesser of the two devils. I had too much riding on this, to risk it going south. I figured I'd tip you off in case I bit the big one," I told him. "The two of us might have some beef, but I couldn't take down Nerezza on my own."

"That almost sounded like gratitude," Hill said with a smile.

I continued to look down at the boiling vat below, not wanting to make eye contact with him.

"You're a lousy friend, Clive...but you're a damn good cop," I admitted.

Hill raised an eyebrow. "Coming from you, that's...something."

As I turned to walk away, my leg nearly collapsed from under me—Luckily for me, Hill caught me before I followed Nerezza to the grave.

"Easy, Guy. You're in bad shape. I wasn't going to say anything, but you look like hell," he said, bracing me up. "Let's get you off this catwalk before you go over too."

True to his word, Hill helped me down the staircase. I was able to stand on my own once we reached ground level.

"You need a ride?" Clive asked. "I could have one of my cars drive you home."

I shook my head. "I'm fine. Got a dame waiting for me back at the office and a couple of wedding bells just waiting to be rung."

"Well, how about that," he said, extending a hand. "Congratulations."

I shook it briefly, then limped over to the spot where Agresta had knocked me out and picked my hat up off the floor.

"You in the market for a best man?"

A fraction of a smile appeared on the less swollen side of my mouth at the thought—though, I pretended I hadn't heard him.

"Take care of yourself, Hill," I said, tipping the brim of my hat.

"You too, Duncan. Be seeing you."

After we parted, I slowly limped out of the factory and out into the rain, over to where I'd parked my car. It was right where I left it.

I started the engine and drove back to the office.

For all I knew, Kat was probably still waiting up for me and, truth be told, I was just as eager to see her after the night I had.

CHAPTER 18

More Than a Catnap

It was still dark when I returned to the office; the sun wouldn't be up for at least a few more hours. The heavy rain outside had not let up and it looked like it would continue its descent, well into the day.

I was surprised to find all the lights in the office turned off. After retrieving the keys from the depths of my pocket, I unlocked the front door and twisted the knob open.

My hand found a switch on the wall, which illuminated the room once I flipped it. I tiredly hung my dripping trench coat on the coat rack beside Kat's and yawned.

I was thankful most of the swelling around the injured parts of my body had started going down. Most of the bruised parts hurt like hell but were still tolerable. I was tired but ready to finally put the nightmare with Capone to rest.

I glanced over at Kat's desk; she was asleep in the desk chair, with her head resting against her shoulder and her body facing the window. It looked like she had nodded off sometime during the night while waiting for me to return. I had half a mind to get a bit of shut-eye myself before we headed over to the courthouse.

She was sleeping so peacefully that I didn't want to wake her. I debated whether or not to let her rest for a few minutes longer, but we had a busy day ahead of us, so it was probably in our best interest to get a start on it together.

With a sigh, I walked over to Kat and spun her around so that she was facing me. I got a clear view of the wedding dress she'd picked out; a beautiful hourglass-shaped dress made of rayon. The dress had a high neckline with decorative rows of buttons and panels of lace sewn into it, which accented it nicely. Her auburn hair was draped over her face.

I was amazed at how well the ivory dress hung on her slender body. She looked even more beautiful in it than when I'd seen her earlier. Clearly, she was just as eager to wear it, as I was to see her in it.

"Kat...Kitten..." I whispered softly, "Time to wake up."

As I gently brushed her hair out of her face, I was met with a pair of lifeless blue eyes.

The shock of the sight caused me to stagger backward. I can't begin to tell you what was going through my head at that moment.

At first, I thought my eyes were playing tricks on me—a hallucination, concocted by either my drowsy state or one too many fists to my noodle—anything but what I was seeing. I didn't want to believe it.

"Kat? Kat!" My tone became more urgent as I attempted to shake her awake. "Talk to me, doll!"

But Kat didn't respond. Her blue eyes—which once held a vibrant abundance of life—only stared off into the void. I checked her wrist for a heartbeat but found none.

Defeated, I dropped to my knees and was overcome with grief. My aching body paled in comparison to the pain tearing me apart from the inside. I wanted to shout—to purge the agony from my body—but found I had neither the physical strength nor the will to do so.

Kat's body slumped forward in the chair and remained still. I discovered the back of her dress was stained with blood from the shoulders down. The blood was almost dry, which meant she had died recently.

I slowly lowered her body to the floor and cradled it in my arms. Her limp arms hung uselessly at her sides as I held her. There were tears in the corner of my eyes, but they refused to run down my bruised cheeks. My mind was trying to process the whole ordeal.

Another wave of grief washed over me, as I suddenly remembered that Kat had not been the only casualty of my misfortune; the unborn child that I had only recently learned existed, was gone too. Any hope of a life with Kat and the family that could have been had died with her.

The warmth of her skin had gone cold. The sudden slumber that had overtaken Kat was far more than a catnap—it was the big sleep that she would never wake up from.

I could not bring myself to stare into her lifeless eyes any longer. It's a sight that will haunt me to the end of my days.

Using my thumb and index finger, I slowly pulled her eyelids shut and drew her head close to my chest; a few droplets of her blood dripped onto my shirt and mixed with the stains my dried blood had left on the fabric.

Peering down at her face, I noticed the makeup near her eyes had left streaked lines down her cheeks; Kat had been crying before she died. The next thing I noticed after brushing her hair to the side, was an entry wound in her forehead—*identical* to the wound I had seen on Lexi Desiree in the morgue. A bullet had been the clear cause of death in both cases.

A dried puddle of crimson stained the floor beside her desk. Whoever killed Kat had shot her at close range—as indicated by the burn marks left by the gunpowder—and then moved her body from the floor to the chair, to make it appear that she was only sleeping at first glance.

My nostrils picked up the scent of *lavender* in the air. I found that strange, given that Kat had an allergy to the small herb and avoided any beauty products that used it. The only explanation for this was that the killer had used the scent to cover the stench of the body if it had not been found until later in the day—but my mind was far too exhausted to put much more thought into that hunch.

I went through the list of suspects in my head; mostly local gangsters and droppers. One name continued to surface: *Marcus Wyant.*

A mixture of rage and grief filled my chest at the thought of Wyant. I had done the job for Capone to protect Kat from getting hurt and none of it mattered in the end.

The thought of Wyant murdering the woman I loved, played over and over again in my mind. I clenched my fists in rage as I recalled each and every threat he made to her. I pictured the smug smile on his ugly face—it made me physically sick.

As I contemplated all the ways I wanted to end Wyant, I suddenly felt all the energy drain from me as I remembered Kat's body. I let out a sigh and unclenched my fists.

For a moment, I had a handle on my rage and pushed it down to unbottle at a later date. It was not the time to lose my head. I looked down at Kat and let the familiar taste of bitterness and hopelessness, fill me once again. It numbed my senses.

My head dropped solemnly. I slowly ran my index finger across the cheek of the woman in my arms; her skin was still as smooth as silk, but it was cold to the touch. Colder still was the undeniable truth that no amount of warmth would ever thaw the chill that death had left on the poor girl. All of it was my fault.

"I'm...I'm sorry you got caught up in my mess..." I said softly to both Kat and the unborn child that never stood a chance, "You both deserved better than what I gave you. I should've done more to keep you safe. Even if I had, everything probably would've flopped apart sooner or later.

"I've been kidding myself. I'm not a good man...I'm beginning to doubt I ever was. I've lied, cheated, murdered, and kept things from you that I shouldn't have...Looking back now, some of those things probably would've given you a fighting chance. If I told you sooner, maybe you'd both still be alive.

"I'm as much a devil as the rest of the filth in this city. I've hurt people for a devil far worse than me. I should've known that eventually my demons would catch up to me in the end—I just never thought they'd find me this soon."

THE DEVIL YOU KNOW

The lump of grief in my throat continued to grow. I forced myself to look at what the fruits of my labors had sewn.

"You were the only good thing in this dark world, doll. I wanted to give you the life you deserved. When all this was over, I was ready to pack up everything and catch the first train going as far away from this city as possible. I wanted to find somewhere I could start again and be the man you thought I was. I let you down."

I sat in silence for a minute and let my failures hang in the air before I continued:

"I should be the one lying dead on the floor—not you. You shouldn't have had to pay the price for all the sins I'm guilty of. The only sin you've ever been guilty of is falling for me.

"Somehow, you've managed to find the last ounce of humanity buried deep inside me and held onto it. You've had the best parts of me from the moment you walked into my life...Those parts will stay buried with you. Out of all the dames in this city, you were the only one worthy of them.

"There's no redemption for me anymore, Kat...any chance of that died with you. You've left me with only the darkest parts of myself that I kept hidden from you. Whatever is left of me is a far cry from the man you loved.

"Maybe, you would've been safer if you never walked through my door. You'd be alive and I'd still be just as low as I am now—minus the heartbreak. You would've been better off without me.

"Once again, the people closest to me end up getting caught in the crossfire. Capone should've never used you to get to me. You deserved so much better than this."

I slowly set Kat's lifeless body on the floor. Her soul was crossing through the Big Pearly Gate in the Sky with the rest of the angels—a place I know I'll never enter. No amount of salvation could save me from my wicked ways. I would never be reunited with Kat when I bought the big one. My soul was bound for somewhere else entirely.

An unquenchable thirst filled my mouth. I wanted a bottle of something to fill the hole Kat had left behind—I didn't even care if it was poison—but my office was as dry as a desert.

After getting to my feet, I grabbed the telephone on Kat's desk and had the operation connect me with the station. The woman answering the telephones at the station told me that Hill had only just returned to the office, but after some convincing, she forwarded my call to him.

"This is Hill," he answered in a tired yet commanding tone.

"Hill, it's Duncan. Get over to my office as soon as you can. There's been another murder..."

CHAPTER 19

Ghosts and Demons

Clive Hill arrived in my office within the hour. When he entered, he was accompanied by two other cops and a coroner. I noticed that one of the badges was carrying a camera with him to snap some photographs of the crime scene to review later back at the clubhouse.

"No one comes in or out of this building without my say-so. Understand?" the detective told another cop in the hallway.

A couple of uniformed bulls passed by my door and continued on to block off all the exits, while Hill went to work. I was sure the killer had long since fled the scene before I had even found Kat's body, but Hill was just following the usual protocols.

Hill walked toward me with the three other men; all of them were dressed for the wet weather and dripping water all over the floor. He gestured to his companions:

"Duncan, this is Officer Douglas and Officer Wayne. They've agreed to assist me with the investigation. I've also brought our coroner, Patrick Wallace, to help inspect and transfer the body once we've wrapped things up here.

"I know this is a difficult time for you, but if you could walk us through what exactly happened when you found the body, it will help us with this investigation."

"Mind telling us where you were last night?" Wayne asked in a sour tone; he had not been present during the raid on Nerezza's factory, as far as I could tell.

Hill quickly turned to the young officer. "He was with me, helping me bust the bootlegging operation that Alastor Nerezza was running down by the docks. I can vouch for that."

The younger cop nodded his understanding, effectively crossing my name off the list of suspects.

"What happened when you arrived here this morning?" Hill asked. "Don't spare any details. I want to hear whatever you can tell me about this mess."

As I recounted everything that happened from the moment I entered my office to the moment I telephoned the station, Hill jotted my statement down in his little notebook. While that was going on, the two other officers spread out. Wayne snapped some photographs of the crime scene, while Douglas searched for any evidence he could uncover.

Once I concluded my statement, Hill asked:

"...And at any point did you move the body?"

I shifted a little as I recalled my mistake, cursing myself under my breath. I'd been sloppy. Instead of leaving Kat's body where I found it, I'd let my emotions get the better of me.

"I...might've," I admitted.

Hill and the coroner shot each other a surprised look.

"You moved the body?"

"Well, not intentionally," I added, "I got caught up in the whirlwind of everything... When I realized she was..."

I couldn't bring myself to finish the sentence, doing so would've made the fact that Kat was dead true.

Hill frowned.

"You realize that moving the body, even unintentionally, could be classified as tampering with a crime scene. I could arrest you for that," he stated.

The dick took a deep breath and let the harshness in his voice evaporate.

"...But, given the shocking nature of the situation — your reaction was a natural one. Grief can make even the most rational person forget things like *protocol*. I'll not hold it against you this time, Duncan. Consider this a freebie." He shook his head. "Where was the body when you first discovered it?"

"In the chair," I answered, pointing at the seat behind Kat's desk.

Hill glanced over at the puddle of dried blood on the floor beside it.

"She wasn't on the floor when you found her?"

I shook my head. "No. Whoever killed Kat wanted it to look like she was asleep when I walked in. They must've moved her from the floor and propped her up in the chair before they fled the scene."

Hill added the new information to his notes. When he finished scribbling some lines down, he approached Kat's body with the coroner.

"Hmm...She was crying before she was killed," he observed, before turning to the coroner. "Any chance she was tortured?"

The coroner inspected Kat's body carefully. "Doesn't look like it. Other than the cause of death, I don't see any other wounds that suggest she was tortured, or even bound when she was killed."

Hill rubbed his chin. The cause of death was as clear as crystal.

"Looks like the bullet that killed her was fired at close range." He looked around the room. "Doesn't look like there was a struggle either."

The dick turned to Douglas and Wayne. "You got enough pictures of everything?"

Wayne nodded.

"Any evidence?"

The two cops looked at each other, before looking back at Hill.

"We got as much evidence as we could find. There wasn't much, but at least we have something to go off of," Douglas said.

"All right," Hill said, "pack up whatever you found and get it back to the station. Hopefully, we'll find something else once the photographs develop.

"In the meantime, we should move the body to the station."

He turned to me.

"Does she have any next of kin that we may need to get in touch with?"

I shook my head. "No. Just me."

The only family I remember her mentioning had been her parents, who had each gotten sick and died a month apart from each other, a little over a year ago. Their deaths had been part of the reason Kat had moved here. Other than that, there was no one else.

THE DEVIL YOU KNOW

"That's too bad..." Hill sighed. "I hate to do this to you, Duncan, but I'm afraid you'll have to come with us."

A short time later, the coroner covered Kat's body with a white sheet. He and another cop carried her body out of the office on a stretcher and loaded it into the back of the coroner's truck. I rode with Hill in his car down to the station. The entire ride, I couldn't get the image of Kat being carried away out of my brain.

I spent most of the day down at the station, answering a bunch of questions that Hill assured me would help with the investigation—I already knew who the killer was, but it would take more than finger-pointing to get any charges to stick on Wyant without the hard evidence that tied him to the murder—my word alone was not enough cause to arrest a man as well connected as him.

We kept going around in circles, even with my cooperation, but nothing was done to bring Wyant in for questioning. The entire time I was there, the only thing I could think about as the hours dragged on, was how Kat and I would've already been hitched by then if she were still alive. The thought offered little to comfort my guilty conscience. Kat's killer was still out there and I was wasting my time answering all their stupid questions.

By the time I finished answering their questions, most of the day had been spent. Hill drove me back to the office and followed me back upstairs. He lit a cigarette once we were back in my office and stared out the window at the rain. The heavy bags under his eyes made him almost look as tired as I was—but then again, he didn't look like he'd been hit by a truck. Still, he wore the troubles of the day on his face like a bad necktie.

The dick puffed slowly one more time before he spoke:

"Hell of a day…"

"Hell of a day…" I repeated.

It felt like the kind of day the Devil himself had planned out—in a way, he had. I took a seat at my desk and lit a cigarette for myself, but the only thing I could think about was Kat's absence in the silence of the office.

"Listen, Guy…I can't begin to imagine what you're feeling right now," Clive said, keeping his gaze out the window. "Of all the days for someone to—well, it can't be easy. Life has a way of kicking a man to the curb, just when he thinks he's found his footing."

He finally turned around.

"I never had the pleasure of meeting Kat in person, but when I talked to her on the telephone, she seemed like a sweet girl. I can see why you liked her. It doesn't seem fair that life has a nasty habit of robbing the world of good people like that. I guess what I'm trying to say is, I'm sorry for your loss."

I didn't say anything in response. I only stared at the vacant desk where Kat once sat and puffed my cigarette silently.

"It sounded like she was cut from a finer cloth than most of the dames in this city," Clive continued. "She must've been a special lady if her...*passing*, is hitting you this hard."

When I didn't respond, he continued:

"I know everything's still fresh and you're going to need time to process it all, but I'm here if you need to talk."

I continued to fix my gaze on Kat's empty desk in the other room.

Clive took that as his cue to leave.

"I can see you need some time to yourself. So I'm just going to—"

"She was carrying my child..." I finally said. "We were going to get out of this place and start a family away from all this."

Hill shook his head. "Shit, Guy...I didn't know."

"No one did. I only found out yesterday."

Clive's full attention was on me. The downward spiral began.

"It should be me lying down at the morgue. Her death is on my hands. She's dead because of me!"

In a sudden outburst, I shoved everything off my desk. The telephone and everything else on it, came crashing to the floor.

My despair quickly turned to rage.

"I know who did this, Hill! He's the same punk who killed Alexis Desiree! I'm going to find the bastard and make him pay!" I shouted.

Clive eyed me carefully—not out of suspicion, but because he knew better than to approach me while I was all riled up.

"I've seen that same look on a thousand faces," he said. "You look like a man bent on doing something he's going to regret. That's not a path you want to go down, trust me. There's no coming back from it.

"Now, I'm willing to admit, there are more than a few similarities between your girl and the Desiree-girl's murders—it can't be a coincidence—but, you're not a cop anymore. You can't just take matters into your own hands because some thug killed your dame. That'll land you in the can.

"Let me handle this. I promise I'll do what I can to make sure Kat gets justice—but if you do what I think you're going to do, then I can't help either of you."

I didn't need Hill's help. He wanted to bring Wyant in still breathing—with all the connections Capone had, Wyant would most likely walk free before he ever saw the inside of a courtroom. There would be no justice for Kat or Lexi then.

The only way to make sure Wyant never hurt anyone again, was to put a bullet right between his eyes. I didn't want him alive. The only justice I'd accept, was when I was standing over his dead body.

Hill headed for the door.

"Think about what I said. I hope to God you don't end up throwing it all away..."

He turned the knob and exited with the tip of his hat.

"Take care of yourself, Duncan."

For the first time all day, I was alone with my thoughts. My mind was already made up. Nothing was going to talk me out of it.

I peered out the window and waited for Hill's car to pull away. When it did, I reloaded my pistol and headed out the door. The thirst that had been building up in my mouth since this morning, was aching for attention and I knew exactly the kind of place that would satisfy it.

After locking up and heading downstairs, I started on the long trek from my office and made my way here, in the pouring rain, with only my ghosts and demons to keep me company.

CHAPTER 20

A Stiff Drink and a Smoking Gun

I took a long drink from my glass of hooch, as I finished telling Sam my story. During its entirety, the two of us had killed five bottles of the good stuff. Judging by the way the dark-skinned man was swaying in his seat, I could tell he was at his limit. I, on the other hand, was able to hold my liquor much better—I had more than a few years of practice when it came to looking at the inside of a bottle than he did.

Hammett brought over another bottle from behind the bar and set it on the table.

"Christ, man! No more!" Sam said in disgust, looking down at the bottle. "Get me a cup of joe. Make it black."

I grabbed the unopened bottle before the old bartender could pick it up and placed it in the inner pocket of my coat for safekeeping. Sam looked at me like I was mad for even considering drinking any more of the stuff, but he didn't try and stop me either.

He took a long moment to reflect deeply on the story I'd told him.

"That's a hell of a sob story," he finally said. "It's a shame what happened to your dame. Honestly. My condolences."

He took a sip of the steaming beverage that Hammett brought over and leaned forward on the edge of his seat. The tone in his voice dropped:

"This city has an abundance of devils running it—not all of them are gangsters neither. I'm glad to hear you were able to put a couple of them *six feet under*. If you ask me, we got enough trash littering our streets—sounds like you did this city a favor."

"Got my hands plenty dirty doing it," I told him, lighting a fresh cigarette. "I'm beginning to think I lost part of myself along the way."

Sam nodded understandingly. "Sounds like you did."

He quickly looked from side to side, to make sure no one else was listening in:

"What about that Lola-girl? You think Capone did her too?"

I shrugged. "Don't know. Haven't seen her since yesterday. I don't care one way or another. The less I see of her, the better. That broad was nothing but trouble."

Sam gestured over to where Wyant was standing, over at the bar. He was busy bumping gums with a dame half his age. She had her arm curled around him like she was getting a nice roll of green for doing it—which, she probably was.

"What're you going to do about Wyant? I could make a call to the clubhouse and let that pal of yours with the badge know he's here. You wouldn't need to lift a finger."

I shook my head. "No. This is personal."

I glanced around the room at the crowd; none of these fools had any idea what was really going on in the shadows of this city. Many were either drinking or dancing their troubles away without a care in the world, oblivious of how lucky they were to be so ignorant.

Sam looked at me confused.

"You just said that you're off the hook with Capone," he pointed out. "Just walk away and let the coppers handle this."

I shook my head. Sam didn't understand the con I'd been fed for years. He couldn't unless he'd been in the same boat himself.

"You're never square with Capone, even when you are," I said. "He always finds some dirt on you that he can use to keep you in the gutter with the rest of the mud. There's no getting out of it."

I'd be lying if I said that part of me hadn't considered taking Sam's advice for a brief moment and just walked away. That was before Wyant spotted me as I stood up from the table to leave.

"Duncan!" he called from across the room, without giving the dame beside him a second thought. "Heard you finally finished the job."

Wyant strode over to where I was standing and left the dame waiting alone at the bar. There'd be no clean sweep for me now.

"...Only took a little arm twisting to get it done."

His wicked smile was full of charm and deceit.

I felt my blood begin to boil. He was so close, that I could smell the dame's perfume all over him—her *lavender* perfume.

"Hey, while I've got you here, the boss has another job for—"

Before he could finish, I drew my loaded Savage and squeezed the trigger.

THE DEVIL YOU KNOW

BANG!

The bullet struck him in the stomach.

The dame he'd been with, screamed loudly at the sight.

The whole joint suddenly went silent. Everyone had their eyes glued on me and Wyant.

The thug barred his teeth at me, as a dark red stain soaked into the fabric of his clean suit. He dropped to his knees and glanced down at the wound in his gut. Anger filled his eyes.

"Son of a bitch! You shot me!" Wyant growled through the pain. "I'm going to—"

BANG!

I fired again; the second bullet passed through his hand and embedded itself into his chest, as he moved to draw his gun. The force of the gunshot knocked Wyant onto his back. To my surprise, he was still alive.

The second shot sent the onlookers into a panic; many of them dived for cover, while others ran as far from the scene as their legs would carry them.

Wyant was furious.

"When Capone hears about this—"

BANG!

I fired another shot; this time, at his arm. I wanted him to suffer before I killed him. What was most frightening about it all was, that I was enjoying it.

"That wife of yours is dead!" the wounded thug roared, "You hear me? Dead!"

I looked down at him, as any stray thoughts of mercy left me.

"I know..." I said coldly and pointed my pistol at Wyant's head before I pulled the trigger one last time.

BANG!

I watched Wyant's body go limp in a puddle of his own blood.

"...That's for Kat."

With Kat's death avenged, I turned away from the body and slowly walked toward the exit.

Sam was on his feet.

"What the hell, Duncan!" he yelled, "Do you know what you just did? Capone's going to kill you when he finds out about this!"

"I already died once today..." I told him, as I continued toward the door, "...the second time shouldn't be so bad."

Without another word, I exited Sam's joint and stepped out into the pouring rain with the smoking Savage still warm in my hand.

CHAPTER 21

The Devil You Know

I returned to the office with the unopened bottle of hooch in hand. The place was far gloomier without Kat in it. Everything there reminded me of her: the framed picture of her parents she kept on her desk; the lush potted Ficus tucked in the corner that she watered religiously every three days; the Underwood typewriter she worked so diligently at; There was almost nowhere in the office that didn't provoke some memory of Kat—the blood-stained floor didn't help either.

After hanging my coat and hat on the rack next to hers, I stumbled over to my desk, and plopped down in my chair, ignoring the mess I'd made earlier during my sudden outburst. I didn't even bother grabbing a glass from the drawer. I drank it straight from the bottle, throwing discretion to the wind. At that moment, I didn't care if someone caught me hitting the bottle, I just wanted to numb every ounce of pain coursing through my body—especially, the pain wracking my mind.

As I drank my sorrows away, I found little solace in knowing I had gunned down the man who'd murdered Kat.

Eventually, I passed out at my desk.

There were no dreams in the blackness, just an empty void of nothingness. I deserved that much. A man like me doesn't deserve the luxury of finding an escape in my sleep.

While my mind continued to float through the endless darkness, I faintly heard the hallway door open. The sound of footsteps soon followed.

As the footsteps grew closer, I drew my Savage and pointed it at the intruder without lifting my heavy head off the desk.

"What do you want?"

A soft voice answered:

"Guy?"

I knew the voice well.

"I don't remember inviting you in, Lola?"

I slowly lifted my head up, keeping my pistol pointed at her the entire time. The grogginess slowly let up and the shape of a woman came into focus in the dark room.

Lola was wearing her black raincoat and a matching hat that covered most of her blonde hair. Both items were completely drenched with rain. She held her black handbag tightly, as she took a step closer.

I noticed she had decorated her face with makeup for this visit. Her lipstick was a dark shade of rose, with lips that were begging to be kissed. Even in her wet get-up, my eyes were still drawn to her. Her shapely legs swayed sensually with each step she took.

"Well, the door was unlocked, so I figured I'd make myself comfortable."

I was almost certain that I'd locked the front door the moment I got back, but it didn't make much difference. She was already in my office. Lola continued:

"Anyway, while I was reading the paper this morning, I noticed that Alastor Nerezza turned up dead after a police raid on his factory. I wanted to check on you and make sure you were okay. It looks like Otis did a number on your handsome face, Love."

"You might want to get your eyes checked if you're talking about my mug," I said.

She smiled flirtatiously. "I like it. It's very devil may care."

Leave it to a pretty dame to lie right to your face and pass it off as a compliment. Lola had perfected the art. She was after something.

"Now that Nerezza's dead," she said, "I was wondering if you found out anything about my sister's killer."

I nodded. "You won't have to worry about that anymore. It's been taken care of."

A look of relief washed over her face.

"Oh thank goodness." she sighed, "What a relief. I'm so happy, I could kiss you."

"I'd rather you didn't," I said, lowering my pistol.

"I'd like the chance to show you my gratitude," she teased, raising a thin eyebrow.

"You want to thank me? Then, why don't you start by coughing up the rest of the money you owe me for the job you hired me to do, and get the hell out of my life? I'm not interested in anything else you have to offer."

Lola looked confused. She was not the kind of girl who got turned down often.

"That's not what you were saying the other night..."

"The other night was a mistake."

The dame shook her head and smiled. "You seemed pretty satisfied to me. Just admit it, you liked it."

I kept my trap shut before I dug myself into a hole I couldn't climb out of. Lola was trying to get a rise out of me. The less I entertained the idea, the easier it would be to keep turning the offers down.

The blonde didn't want to take "no" for an answer.

"We could do it again...Right here, in this office..." she proposed. "If we hurry, your wife will never find out."

That was the first time I'd thought about Kat since Lola stepped into my office. With all the webs of seduction being spun, I'd almost forgotten about Kat's death.

"Of course, she won't..." I agreed, "she's dead."

The news didn't seem to surprise the blonde woman.

"Oh, is that so? That's too bad. Sorry to hear that, Love." She looked away for a moment. "Seems like innocent girls dying, are a dime a dozen these days. Maybe it just wasn't meant to be."

The apathy in her voice made the words seem less than genuine. She looked at me with her hand resting on her hip. I was disgusted by the shameless attempt.

"You've got some nerve, sister. Talking about Kat like that when she hasn't even been dead for twenty-four hours. Your bedside manner could use some work."

"Sorry," she lied and opened her handbag. "Do you mind if I smoke?"

When I shook my head, she reached into her bag and pulled out a box of smokes. After that, she placed a fresh one past her lips and burned the tip of the roll with her lighter. A puff of smoke slowly escaped her lips.

"Thank you," she nodded, then continued, "All I'm saying is that, maybe her death doesn't need to be such a bad thing."

"How do you figure that?"

Lola smiled and stared at me with those icy-blue eyes.

"It gives us a chance to be together," she said bluntly. "Don't you see? With your *squeeze* out of the way, we don't have to keep sneaking around anymore. I can have you all to myself."

Something about the way Lola was talking smelled off—Come to think of it, her story wasn't the only thing that smelled.

"Interesting perfume you're wearing tonight," I said, dodging the subject. "What's the occasion?"

The blonde let out a small laugh. "Now, Guy, you of all people should know that a girl never needs a reason to wear perfume for her man."

She took a step closer to me. I immediately recognized the scent: *lavender perfume.* I gripped my pistol tighter but kept it low. The pieces fit together. It was at that moment I realized I'd killed the wrong person. Wyant hadn't killed Kat, Lola had.

The anger began to surge within me, but I decided to let Lola keep believing I was still in the dark about it. Sooner or later, she'd slip up and confess her crime.

"What kind of perfume is that?" I asked, already knowing the answer.

"*Lavender Rose*," Lola said proudly. "You like it?"

"It's not terrible," I admitted. "The only issue I got with it is that I smelled it earlier...when I found Kat dead in my office."

Cracks were beginning to form in the facade Lola had created; still, she continued playing the part of the innocent dame.

"She has good taste in perfume, then. She probably put some on last night, while she was waiting for you," the blonde said; she could tell I wasn't convinced. "Honestly, Love, it sounds like you're looking for devils, where there are none.

"It's understandable. I wouldn't trust anyone either if I found the person I loved dead at their desk."

Lola had just slipped up. It was time to uncover the truth.

"Kat was allergic to lavender..." I told her, "...and, I never mentioned that she was at her desk when I found her."

The smile on Lola's face vanished. She eyed me bitterly.

"I wish you hadn't noticed that, Love..."

In a flash, she reached into her handbag and drew her pistol. Before I could lift my arm, Lola pulled the trigger.

BANG!

The bullet struck me in the chest, just below the heart. I fell backward out of my seat—my pistol tumbled out of reach when I hit the floor.

"Look what you made me do!" Lola waved her pistol around angrily. "It wasn't supposed to be this way! You should've forgotten about the moll in your office and run away with me!"

I groaned in pain, as I slowly propped my injured body against the wall in a sitting position on the floor. Blood quickly soaked through my shirt. I applied pressure to the wound and looked up at Lola.

"I should've known. You were the one who killed Kat."

Lola smiled triumphantly. "I did. That bim was getting in the way of us. I wanted her dead the moment I saw you two making eyes at each other. It made me sick! It should've been me you were looking at, not her!

"After all these years, I waited long enough for a second chance with you! I wasn't going to let some pencil-pusher take that chance away from me!"

"So when you hired me to track down your sister, it never had anything to do with reconnecting with her, did it?" I said, "You just used her as an excuse to con your way back into my life."

"Oh no, Love, you played your part perfectly. I knew Agresta would never leave me alone with my sister at the party—not after he found out I was working for his boss too. He didn't want Lexi getting caught up in any of this. Must've been afraid that I'd spill the beans on what he was really doing while working those late nights if she and I ever talked."

I had to backtrack, just to make sure I'd heard Lola correctly.

"You work for Nerezza?"

"*Worked...*" she corrected, "I *worked* for Nerezza."

She saw my puzzled expression.

"A girl's got to eat, Love, and I have *very* expensive tastes these days..." she frowned, "Though, it's hard to get paid when your employer turns up dead on the front page of the morning paper."

The blonde caught herself getting distracted:

"Anyway, Nerezza thought that Agresta was getting soft—at one point it seemed like he was considering going straight for my sister and leaving his life of crime behind. She was a distraction, you see. Nerezza didn't like to see his top muscle pulling his punches—made him look soft too. He wanted her out of the picture for good, without Agresta finding out."

"So he hired you to kill her for him..." I finished, "...your own sister."

A disgusted scowl appeared on Lola's face. "Alexis and I grew apart a long time ago. She didn't want to talk to me for a few months after she heard how things ended between us. Blamed me for what happened, instead of taking my side. Our relationship never really recovered after that.

"I hadn't seen her in months. She was more of a familiar stranger than a sister to me.

"When she left, I had no one for a very long time. Then, from out of nowhere, Nerezza comes along and makes sure all the bills are paid, keeps the lights on, and such, in exchange for a few favors. He told me he'd keep the money coming if I used my feminine wiles to get close to his competition and woo them into doing business.

"If they weren't playing ball with him, he'd send me to kill them when he wanted someone dealt with, discreetly. I'd been doing it for a while when he asked me to kill Lexi."

I couldn't help but see myself in her story. As much as I hated to admit it, we had a lot more in common than I thought—didn't change the fact that she was still pointing a pistol at me. Either way, I'd been duped into leading Lola right to her sister. I felt dirtier than I'd felt after sleeping with her.

"After our little argument that night, I tailed Lexi when she left the Drake, while you were being led upstairs to Nerezza's office. Because Agresta was preoccupied with you, he didn't even notice Lexi slip away from the party.

"Killing Lexi was duck soup. Once I followed her into an alley and shot her, I knew the cops would pass it off as a mugging. The real challenge was making *you* believe I was grieving my sister's death—I practiced in front of a mirror, and everything—and you bought it."

She was right. I'd fallen for her sob story hook, line, and sinker.

"After I killed Lexi, I returned to Nerezza. He told me he wanted me to keep an eye on you and find out what you'd collected on him. If I'm being completely honest, I was more than happy to be spending more time with you.

"The following day, I noticed the files you had on your desk and saw exactly where you kept them. You practically gift-wrapped them for me. I let Nerezza know you were getting too close to uncovering what he was running down at the docks. He wanted those files badly."

Realization slapped me across the face like an angry broad. "You were the one who jimmied the locks and stole the files from my office."

Lola nodded. "Initially, I was just going to steal the files, deliver them to Nerezza, and then disappear, but then I saw how you were around that secretary of yours. I wanted you all to myself.

"Believe it or not, I actually missed you, after things ended between us. So I snuck into your apartment and reminded you just how much I wanted you back," she frowned. "After all that, you still wanted to be with that floozy."

A wicked smile slowly curled the ends of her lips.

"I can't say my efforts were completely wasted. That night, I made you guilty of all the sins that you accused me of, the night you caught me with Hill.

"As much as you try to deny it, you are just as much a devil as I am now. You should have seen the way your fiancée cried when I told her about that night and what we did. It broke her heart—then, I ended her life. It's almost poetic."

I was losing a lot of blood. It was becoming increasingly harder to focus on what was happening, but I couldn't let myself nod off just yet. Lola was giving me everything—everything except, justice for Kat's murder.

"So..." I coughed; a bit of blood formed at the corner of my mouth. "You killed my girl because I picked her over you."

"I was your girl first!" Lola spat. "She had no right to you!"

"She was carrying my child!" I roared.

Lola had not been expecting to hear that. Her eyes widened with confusion and surprise. It seemed like it was genuinely the first time she was hearing about it.

"Your... child?... I-I didn't know..."

I coughed some more:

"Neither did I...At least, not until the other night. It just happened."

Lola's lip quivered.

"I could've given you one. The only thing I ever wanted was the chance to start over with you," she said, as a heavy tear filled her eye. "I-I love you, Guy."

Her hands were shaking; though, her pistol was still pointed at me.

As I looked up at the dame responsible for ruining my life more times than I could count, I couldn't help but admit how beautiful she was. From the way things looked, Lola's life was almost as much of a trainwreck as mine was.

I wanted to deny that I found my eyes pinned to her, but there was something about the pain behind those icy-blue eyes that kept my gaze drawn to her. I wanted to hate her—to despise her—but, I couldn't.

"After everything you put me through over the years—all the hell and heartache—There's still a small part of me that cares about you. I'd be lying if I said I didn't find myself wondering how things would've played out if things didn't end the way they did between us. Maybe we would've found that happiness we've both been looking for..."

I slowly got to my feet. Apart from a brief dizzy spell, I managed to keep myself upright.

"It's not too late. Give me the gun, Lola..." I begged gently, holding out my free hand, "...Give me the gun and we can make everything right."

I could read the conflict on Lola's face like a bad romance novel. She was trying to decide what she wanted to do. The tears continued to run down her eyes, while she weighed her options.

Carefully and cautiously, I inched my way closer to her, until I was face-to-face with her.

She slowly let her arms drop and surrendered the gun to me.

"There we go..." I said calmly, holding the weapon at my side.

Lola threw her arms around me and sobbed:

"Oh, Guy...I'm so sorry. I didn't want any of this. I just love you so much!"

"I love you too..." I admitted, before pulling her into a kiss.

Her body pressed against mine, as she pulled me closer. Tears of sadness and pain quickly turned to tears of joy. Lola had everything she ever wanted.

BANG!

Lola's blue eyes suddenly went wide in shock, as I broke the kiss.

"...but I loved Kat more," I whispered into her ear.

A mix of confusion and betrayal filled her eyes. She slowly peered down and found her pistol pressed against her chest, held tightly in my hand.

The blonde staggered in place for a moment and inspected the bullet hole to her heart with dainty fingers—blood covered the tips of them. Lola looked at me, one last time, before finally collapsing to the floor.

Kat's killer was dead. The woman I loved could finally rest in peace, knowing I had brought her justice.

I looked down at Lola's beautiful corpse and tossed the smoking gun in my hand aside. My body and soul were as numb as ice. I no longer felt anything for the dead blonde woman at my feet.

I reached over to the half-empty bottle of hooch on my desk and picked it up. Lifting it to my lips and tilting my head back, I took a long gulp of it, until there was none left.

The loss of blood had drained me of all my remaining energy and my legs collapsed from under me, a moment later. My bleeding body slid down the side of the desk, leaving a trail of red behind, until it found the floor.

It was getting harder and harder to keep my eyes open. I was in bad shape—probably didn't have long for this world. I didn't care if I lived or died. I'd already lost everything.

I hadn't pegged Lola as Kat's killer until moments before there was a bullet in my chest—by then, it was too late.

Maybe Lola had been right; Maybe I've always been a devil, like so many others in this city. Who's to say? All I know is, that there is no coming back from the wrong I've done and the devils I've crossed paths with.

It's been said that it's better to deal with the devil you know than the devil you don't—but what they don't tell you, is that sometimes the devil you know is the more dangerous one. Lola was mine; a fallen angel who knew exactly how to hurt me. She walked back into my life with the sole intention of burning it down. I'd been damned from the start.

As the rain continued to fall and the thunder rumbled, the world was getting darker with each passing second. I rested my head back. It was getting harder to keep pressure on my wound, so I just let my arm drop to my side.

If I bled out, what did it matter? I already had plenty of blood on my hands—what difference did it make if I added my own to the list. This was the fate I deserved. Live or die, I was bound for Hell, either way.

I took one last look at Lola's body, before letting everything go black.

About the Author

James Schroeder was born in Palatine, IL in 1991. Growing up in a family of educators, he was always writing stories and other forms of creative writing in his spare time. Throughout his high school and part of his college career, he wrote screenplays for clubs but eventually started writing short stories, instead, for leisure. After writing a handful of longer stories and Fanfiction, Mr. Schroeder decided to write his own original works. His love for the Mystery and Noir genres inspired him to write his novel, The Devil You Know. The Devil You Know is Mr. Schroeder's first book.

Read more at https://www.jamesschroederauthor.com/.